GRANTA

THE DREAMER O

SEAN FRENCH lives in London with the novelist Nicci
Gerrard and four children. He writes a weekly column in
New Statesman & Society and is the author of two biog-
raphies, of Patrick Hamilton and Brigitte Bardot, and one
other novel, *The Imaginary Monkey*, also published by Granta
Books.

SEAN FRENCH

THE DREAMER
OF DREAMS

GRANTA BOOKS
LONDON
in association with
PENGUIN BOOKS

GRANTA BOOKS

2/3 Hanover Yard, Noel Road, London N1 8BE

Published in association with the Penguin Group
Penguin Books Ltd, 27 Wrights Lane, London W8 5TZ, England
Viking Penguin, a division of Penguin Books USA Inc.,
375 Hudson Street, New York NY 10014, USA
Penguin Books Australia Ltd, Ringwood, Victoria, Australia
Penguin Books Canada Ltd, 10 Alcorn Avenue,
Toronto, Ontario, Canada M4V 3B2
Penguin Books (NZ) Ltd, 182–190 Wairau Road,
Auckland 10, New Zealand

Penguin Books Ltd, Registered Offices: Harmondsworth, Middlesex,
England

First published in Great Britain by Granta Books 1995
This edition published by Granta Books 1996

1 3 5 7 9 10 8 6 4 2

Printed in Great Britain by Clays Ltd, St Ives plc

A CIP catalogue record for this book is available from the British Library

To Kersti and Philip French

Dreamer of dreams, born out of my due time,
Why should I strive to set the crooked straight?

William Morris

. . . during the last year of her life, Garland appeared on the Jack Paar television show and spoke bitterly of the Munchkins as 'drunks who got smashed every night.' Her bitterness extended to Haley, Bolger, and Lahr—they had upstaged her, pushed her out of the way, shoved her into the background. Jack Haley, watching the Paar program, sat bewildered in front of his television set, whispering, 'It's untrue. It's untrue.' 'How could you upstage anybody?' he asks. 'For Christ's sake, we were linked arm in arm all the time.'

The Making of the Wizard of Oz
by Aljean Harmetz

Part One

1. Where do donkeys go in winter?

THE LITTLE BOY, who was called Horace Dean and was seven years old, and his father, who was called Henry George Dean and was thirty-seven years old, used to take walks together on Saturday afternoons. This was called (by Henry, grimly) 'giving Lori a rest', and the two of them would bustle purposefully out of the house, leaving her behind them watching the TV or reading the paper. And they would go to see reconstructed models of dinosaurs, old paintings, animals in cages, moon rock.

On each visit, Horace would ask questions, some strange and gnomic, others entirely sensible, and Henry (nobody ever called him Harry) would be unable to answer either kind without resort to obfuscation or even outright mendacity. He would guiltily resolve to look the answers up, indeed to find out about the whole subject so that he would be able to explain who was turning into what on the side of some vase, or identify a bird's song and the other things fathers were meant to know.

The excursions, which were supposed to be educational and good for everybody, had been conceived with high hopes but were now a burden. This Saturday, a dark, unpromising day, Henry hadn't planned anything, which he felt that Horace resented beneath his wrinkled brow, and he tried to convince his son that a walk up to the pond via the shops and then back down on the Heath was an adventure.

'I'll show you where I used to ride on the donkeys when I was just your age,' he had promised, pushing Horace's stiff, rebukingly resistant arms into his duffel coat, its rough grey fabric itself like the matted hide of a donkey.

'Can I have a ride on a donkey?' A dim glow of enthusiasm poked from the embers of a day-long sulk.

'You can if we see any,' Henry had replied recklessly.

As he pushed the toggles of Horace's duffel coat through the loops with his thumb and was concerned that one was left over at the top, though not concerned enough to undo them all and start again, he was struck by conscience and added prudently:

'There may not be any donkeys. I don't think they have them there any more.'

'Why?'

'I don't think they're allowed to any more. Maybe they decided it was too cruel. For the donkeys.'

'Why?'

Henry looked at his son's face and brushed some wisps of hair away from in front of his brown eyes, Lori's brown eyes. Another dominant gene.

'Put that protruding lower lip away,' Henry said.

*

Horace had been led out of the house, disenchanted by the prospect of a pilgrimage to a place where donkeys once had been but no longer were. Stripped of its nominal purpose, the expedition was perilously close to being that forbidden thing, a walk. Horace was capable of covering moderately large distances on foot if he was running from one animal to another, or talking, or imagining himself engaged on a quest—if he was doing something that would cajole him into forgetting what a hard thing it was to place one foot before the other. Today, he had not wanted to go out at all and he immediately began to complain of his tiredness.

'I'm going to show you something very interesting. Just keep walking and you'll see.'

'What is it?'

'You'll see it when you get there,' Henry said.

A game. This was the sort of thing that awakened Horace's interest.

'Is it something I can have? Is it something I can take with me?'

'It's a surprise,' said Henry, who had not yet thought of what it could be.

Horace softened slightly, but in the temporary thaw, Henry found himself unable to explain why the days were shorter in winter than in summer or indeed why it was warmer in summer than in winter. It must be something to do with the equator, because he was sure that days were the same all the year round on the equator, but why would that make them different anywhere else?

Horace quickly saw that his father couldn't answer. Henry felt him stiffen at his side, an uncooperative miniature mannequin, a resistant troll being dragged up the high street.

They began to attract glances from passers-by, and Henry wondered if he was entirely safe. Did they look convincingly like a father and son going out to have fun? Henry felt more like the wicked father in the early part of a fairy tale, taking his son into the forest in order to leave him there. He imagined Horace seeking help from the crowd: *my daddy hits me* or *my daddy forces me* or something. A crowd would be summoned, calls made, his progress blocked by concerned citizens; there would be a firm escort into a car, a cell, interviews with police and with a social worker. Horace prodding bits of a doll at random. The floppy bits and the holes would probably look the most interesting. *He touched me there*, and *he grabbed hold of that* and *he put his finger in that*. It would get all confused with the resentments over the walk. *He told me that if I didn't go all the way with him, Mummy would be sad.* MR EVIL in the tabloids. Years in prison. Solitary confinement, special category, to protect him from the righteous vengeance of the murderers and armed robbers. Sometimes, Henry felt that a long prison sentence in a comfortable prison was just what he needed. Get some reading done, learn another language, write a book. A visit from Lori and Horace once a month. Probably still find a way of not getting anything done.

Horace seemed too sullen even to go to the trouble of denouncing him. Henry had hoisted him up into his arms but he sensed too late that his son really was too large to carry. Horace had become heavy.

Henry could no longer remember, if he was honest with himself, how Horace had looked at the different stages of his three years, except with the help of photographs. But he could remember the feel of his body, what he was like to hold. He had first been an immobile, tiny bundle, folded in on itself, unseeing, unresponsive. Then, the best part really, the bundle had opened up, arms reaching out, and become needy and demanding. Horace would fold into the neck of his father, gripping the shirt or the face with strong little claws. Now he was no longer designed to fit into the folds of an adult human body. Horace's legs were dangling down on either side of Henry's thighs, and his arms draped over Henry's shoulders. To be managed at all, carrying a child Horace's size required active cooperation from the passenger, but Horace was making little effort to stay engaged.

'You're too old for this,' said Henry at one episode of crisis. 'I bet Sonic doesn't have to be carried everywhere by his daddy.'

With a vengefully brisk effort, Henry raised his son further up in his arms, taking the weight in his right elbow with a quarter turn so that his burden was able to face the street. The boy wriggled, painfully, turning up to the porridgy sky or down to the dull cardboard colour of the paving-stones. Henry sought some distraction, for himself as much as for Horace:

'If you could have anything from any of these shops, what would you choose?'

'Are you going to buy me a present?'

There was a sufficient stirring of interest to allow Henry to let Horace slide down his thigh on to the ground.

'No, it's only a game. Imagine you could choose one thing. It could be something huge, or something tiny, something expensive.'

Henry remembered too late that his son was always troubled by games, especially those which demanded some degree of speculation. Already he seemed pained by the multiple absurdities of what he was being called on to do. The tip of his small nose seemed to harden with the effort of concentration.

'If it was too big, we couldn't carry it home.'

'It's a made-up game, Horace. You can take anything you want but it's only in your head. You can imagine it being taken home by magic if you like. Look at all these shops we're going past. There's a beautiful golden jacket, would you like that?'

'That's a jacket for a grown-up.'

'Yes, but you could have it changed by magic so that it would fit you personally. Or there are the pots and pans in that shop, you could have a beautiful pot, if you like.' Henry knew he was losing Horace's interest. He felt himself caught in an improvisation that had gone up the wrong road. Say something, say anything at all. 'What if a wizard came and said that you could have anything you wanted but you had to decide within ten seconds?'

Disaster. Horace's rounded features registered the agony of indecision.

'How long is ten seconds?'

'Oh, you know. You can tell by counting like this: one thousand, two thousand, three thousand, four thousand, five thousand, six thousand and so on up to ten thousand. That's the same as ten seconds.'

'How much is a thousand?'

'It doesn't matter. That's not the point. You just say a thousand to fill up the time so that it takes a second to say it. Now choose something. Just say what you would like from one of these shops. Imagine that a bad wizard had come and said that you could choose any present you wanted from any one of these shops but you had to choose within ten seconds or he would torture you to death. All right then, choose. Starting fro-o-om now. One thousand, two thousand, three thousand.'

Horace started to cry. There was another flutter of concerned glances from passers-by, and Henry sat his son down on the step in the doorway of a shop and fussed over him in a convincingly concerned way. He told him not to be silly and wiped his moist cheek with a hardened lump of kitchen roll that had been left in his pocket when his trousers went through the washing-machine. He undid and accurately redid the toggles on his duffel coat. In seven years, this little thing would be worrying about not having a girlfriend and about dying. Henry had to move Horace aside for a girl in a plastic skirt tight as a sausage skin to clatter past them, rubbing her pelvic area virtually along his nose as she passed, but Henry knew that, as the custodian of a child, he was rendered sexually null in her eyes. Henry led his son on up the hill, hoping Horace would not notice for a while that he wasn't being carried.

'What songs do you know about people going up hills?'

'What ones?'

This was delicate. Horace still liked nursery rhymes, when not in company, but he didn't like the fact to be acknowledged.

'Don't just say what ones. Try and think. You know the one about the people who went up the hill to fetch a pail of water.'

'I knew that,' Horace protested. 'Jack and Jill. You didn't need to give me a clue.'

'And who marched his men up to the top of the hill and then marched them down again?'

'The grandoledukeofYork. I knew that as well. You shouldn't have said that. Of course I knew that.'

'And what about this? Dee dee dee dee dee, dee dee dee dee . . . '

'Music.'

A small burble issued from Horace as a signal that the sulk had temporarily been suspended.

'Foo-ool on the . . . '

'Hill. I knew that.'

Another little farting gurgle escaped, and Henry began a conversation about why people walked up or climbed hills and mountains. He tried to think of the difference between a hill and a mountain; whether the relevant distinction was height, sharpness, rockiness as against greenness. He unsuccessfully attempted to recall small mountains and big hills. He imagined falling off a hill.

Building a mountain. God would never ask you to take your son up to the top of a hill to sacrifice him. Only a mountain would do for something as serious as that. Henry George Dean took his son, Horace Dean, up to the top of the hill and made a pile of wood next to the Whitestone Pond and he took out a knife and made as if to stab his son with it. When he was restrained by onlookers, he insisted that he loved his son dearly but that God had told him to do it. Henry looked at the bulky little figure dragging down once more on his right hand.

'Henry? Why can't I see the stars?'

Henry was distressed by his son's inability to call him by anything but his first name. Lori had always been repelled by the charade of calling each other Mummy and Daddy in front of their child. Say hello to Daddy. Give Mummy a hug. So it was Henry, Lori and Horace, formally addressing each other like three Edwardian friends who happened to be sharing rooms as some matter of personal convenience. He improvised an answer about light being drowned out by light. He searched for a comparison. Water in water, a needle in a haystack. Not quite right. In response to a further interrogation about being unable to see the sky or the clouds, he attempted, with less conviction, to manufacture an answer that shut his son up. Henry was becoming irritated by the successive questions and tired of trying to think why clouds didn't just fall to the ground.

For what cause would he sacrifice his son? Pointless to speculate until the need arose. When it came to a real emergency, perhaps he would be playing the minor role of the person who panics, who leaves his post, betraying his comrades. Horace would be tossed to the savage man-eater in order to give his father a few seconds to make good his escape. Horace would be tossed out of the balloon in order to gain the crucial few feet of height. After all, Horace wouldn't be capable of steering a hot-air balloon to safety. Abraham was rewarded for being willing to murder his son on the say-so of a voice in his head. His seed was multiplied as the stars in heaven. Abraham went all the way to the wire and got the reward, but he never felt quite the same about the God that had demanded this as a test of him. Even street gangs demand only the murder of an outsider by the prospective member, not of the applicant's only son. As for Isaac, he never believed in God again. You have to look out for yourself in this world, was the lesson he drew from the sight of his father standing over him with the knife sharpened at the family's own whetstone. For different reasons, neither of them ever told his mother what had happened during their three days away; she was too old to understand, she might not have appreciated the principle involved. God was left dissatisfied also, despite the apparent success of his experiment. He had not been confident of Abraham's loyalty before and he still wondered whether his servant had done anything more than call his bluff. Abraham had defeated God in the chicken game. He was confident that the author of creation would never allow him to kill his own son. He just had to look as if he was going to do it. And anyway, who would trust a man willing to murder his own son as a favour? Even God was confused.

Henry felt a grey hatred for his surroundings sinking on to him. The lines of cars, wedges of cheese pointing up and down the hill, each with its one stolid-faced occupant, staring into space, listening to trash on the radio, making inordinate efforts to thwart any car from a side road attempting to enter the stream. Is your journey really necessary? In the infrequent buses, the passengers sat, plastic shopping bags on laps, staring in front of them, nothing to read, staving off boredom only by energetically avoiding each other's gaze. On the pavement, the pedestrians—what a word, as if walking were a craft requiring study, a group to which one was granted access—the pedestrians looked lost, bemused. They progressed slowly, dismally, along the street, sometimes staring blankly at a shop window, as if their vision alone could grant ownership; sometimes one of them would wander into a shop, a prosperous woman making herself believe that she needed something new.

A tin was rattled harshly beneath Henry's nose by a gaunt woman in a uniform. He was caught. Slowed down by Horace, he could not plausibly increase his pace and alter his trajectory while pretending to scrutinize the other side of the road. He pushed his hand into the corner of his coat pocket and removed the coins. Pounds, fifties, twenties, tens, fives, twos, ones. He picked out a twenty-pence piece. People will get sentimental about even that one day. Like threepenny bits.

'Here, Horace. Can you put the coin in the tin?'

The woman offered Horace a sticker, and he gravely attached it across the two flaps on his left training shoe.

The people wandering up and down the street,

distracting themselves by staring into windows, spending money, sitting in cafés: how many of them had ever considered the freedom they had to do something different on a Saturday, go and see something else, or indeed change their lives entirely? There was no need to move along in the crowd, and yet there they all were, drifting along together. And so on, thought Henry, bored with his own stream of thought. Blah blah blah.

The houses, the original houses, were different. Behind the bright windows, the stereotyped displays, the bored, insolent assistants misleadingly dressed in the shop's own clothes, behind all the bits that people were actually conscious of, there were the old houses. They were all crammed into a city that was built for other people, a Georgian city demolished and reconstructed by Victorians, streets conceived for hansom cabs and horses, houses designed for families with servants. The more recent attempts to institute new kinds of space are even more disastrous. Walkways and piazzas based on some architectural fantasy, the shopping centres with some fogy's memory of a Georgian roof. We haven't made our own environment, we're just squatting in it, tinkering and making do, not even aware that our consciousnesses are being crushed into something they weren't designed for. Not that the original was much good either. Worse probably. Henry was tired.

It was an unsatisfactory hill to reach the top of, with no sense of release or space, no vista behind, nothing that had been conquered. There were no donkeys.

'Are the donkeys only there in summer?' Horace asked.

'I don't know. We can come back and see when it's hot and sunny.'

Henry's memories of the spot were overlaid with repeated visits over more than thirty years, and memories of those memories. In truth, he couldn't remember whether he had actually ridden on those donkeys or not, or whether he had ever ridden on any donkey. Perhaps he had only been told about the donkeys just as Horace was being told about them. Donkeys were the sort of things that would be ridden on tomorrow, or would have been ridden on had they been there. He led his son along the south side of the pond, glancing to his right at the occasional, partial views across London. The view was disappointingly flat and hazy on this grey winter afternoon. The fragments of the city through the branches of the trees looked vast but nondescript in the distance. This, such as it was, was what he had come for. He hoisted his son right up on to his shoulders and felt the grip on his scalp above each ear as Horace secured his position.

'You're young, Horace, you can do anything you want. That's London down there. The world is yours.'

'I don't want it.'

2. Pessimism of the intelligence; optimism of the will—or should that be the other way round?

IT WAS THE same every night, and this was part of the problem. How would a cinematic version of Henry's life be able to cope with this? Henry would not have described this even to himself as something that plagued him, or even irritated him, but it was a recurrent gnat's bite of unsatisfactoriness. Films, the films that Henry half-watched on television, about American men wearing suits and hats, and people drinking cocktails in nightclubs, consisted of sequential, linear action. About the sort of things that happen once in a lifetime and set it on a new course. Henry, a handsome, young, under-appreciated man, meets a beautiful heiress, and his life is never the same again. There are some obstacles and complications, as he faces the problem of what to do with his wife and child, but when they are suddenly killed in a terrible car crash, he is free to be united with his true love.

Henry's actual existence was never never-the-same-again, but was in fact always a bit more, or a repetition, or, it seemed nowadays, a lesser, attenuated, worn-out version of what he had already been through. For a long time Henry used to go to bed early. Sometimes when he had put out the light on his bedside table—it needed two hands, absurdly, because otherwise the small china base had a tendency to fall off and the bulb would flare up and extinguish—his eyes would close so quickly that he didn't even have time to say to himself: I'm falling asleep. How do you convey that verb on a screen? The movie camera has no past imperfect tense. The significant things in Henry's life were not the anomalies, the odd details that could be recalled, but the habituated, numbed repetitions, the successive days that could no more be recalled individually than the successive layers of butter smeared on Horace's breakfast toast could be separated, as he had once demanded.

'I want one less bit of butter than that,' Horace had said.

A stratum of butter was scraped off the toast.

'That's not the same butter that you put on last. I only wanted the butter that was there before. You spoiled it.'

'Of course it's the same. I took it from the top didn't I? How could it not be the one I put it on last?'

It was no good. Such arguments never prevailed.

Henry spent his mornings aimlessly. How could that be filmed? The traditional method would be the amusing montage. Some music would play, accompanying a series of brief shots: Henry staring into space; Henry making a

27

cup of tea; Henry reading the paper; Henry opening the fridge; Henry drawing shapes on a bit of paper, folding the bit of paper up and launching it across the room; Henry scrunching up the paper and tossing it with concentration towards the waste-paper basket. Missing it. The waste-paper basket standing at the heart of a mound of scrunched-up pieces of paper. Ho ho. End of sequence. Henry planning a film version of his own life. The trouble is that reiteration in a film generally appears not stolidly cumulative, as it is in life, but insane like the bang-bang-bang of a drill. Pondering this problem, Henry thought of one of those period films in which a suitor calls repeatedly with different bunches of flowers for a girl who is 'not at home'. I'm sorry, Mr Fortescue, Miss Smithers is not at home. I'm sorry, Sir. No, still not at home. Finally just a wry shake of the head. What film can't convey is the abstraction of habitual behaviour, the dull indistinguishability of repetition, in which the meaning resides in the pattern, not in the detail of the individual event, experience accumulating like a slag heap. Except perhaps that the slag grows no bigger, except that it occupies more time.

For a long time Horace had gone to bed late, and it had become later and later. His going to bed was an arcane ritual, and he himself was its high priest, presiding over its enactment, supervising the accretion of detail that enlarged it week by week. New habits were adopted, fewer old ones were forgotten and dispensed with. Horace's grasp of the duties and dispensations was precise and dictatorial. It extended back through the passage of his memory, four years at least, before it faded into murky memories of things he had been told about, indistinguishable from things he might have experienced for himself.

The beginning of the end of every day was a downstairs game, the rules of which were divined and communicated by Horace; soft, fleshy folds of concentration at the top of his nose and above his eyebrows, the other lesser players marshalled by his quiveringly extended index finger.

'You sit there, and I sit here, and the bear sits there, and the owl sits there, and you chase me, but if I sit down, you can't chase me, and if I stand on the sofa, you can't chase me and not if I put my hand up. No, don't chase me now, not when we haven't started, and now I'm on the sofa. And we can't start until I say start and I haven't said start yet or until I'm on that chair or on the rug.'

The owl and the bear would remain stationary, and little more freedom was allowed to the game's other participants. On many occasions, no action whatever was permitted, and the game had no existence outside Horace's baroque, improvised rules, as if a country were to exist only in the shadowy, tentative form of a fragmentary map. The recitation itself constituted the game, an accumulation of clauses and sub-clauses punctuated only by the pause for breath and halted in the end only by the brusque, intrusive order to make his way upstairs. After the breakdown of negotiations and the elapsing of a series of deadlines, he would break for the stairs and scuttle up with his stringy toy bear, squashed and worn by an existence of being clutched and squeezed and slept on.

Upstairs, Horace was awaited by the hot, damp fog of the bathroom. The bear was dropped, and he raised his hands up to the ceiling. There might be the pretence of an objection: You can undress yourself. You're a grown-up boy now. But the warmth and wetness lent itself to a collusive fantasy of babyhood. And he was so slow, so likely to start thinking about something on the way, to freeze with his hand on a clasp, that this seven-year-old boy still needed to be undressed so long as none of his friends was around to see. A sweater would be scratched over his face, then the shirt beneath. Sometimes a button would be forgotten and it would catch—irretrievably, it seemed—over the hook of his chin or his nose, blocking his breath for a few seconds. He shrieked and grunted, but all the while comfortingly aware of the expert measures being taken, and he was soon gratefully inhaling the humid air. The mysterious knots were untangled and removed, socks tugged off with a ticklish giggle—do it again! do it again!—trousers kicked away, knickers pulled off. Horace would protest against any aid and would hoist one leg then the other over the rim of the bath and down into the foamy water, Mr Matey grinning down at him from his vantage point behind the taps. Sometimes tamely cool, sometimes too hot, stinging his buttocks, the soft walnut of his balls, and he would hoist himself back up on to the rims, a single-span fleshy bridge over the water, until the imbalance was redressed.

Primary plastic colours glimmered around him, the unsatisfactory bath toys. The rough, brown, heavy ducks he was taken to see in the park floated effectively enough, their splayed triangular feet flapping beneath them, dim in the brown water. Did real ducks' feet get cold? Did real ducks ever topple over? However carefully Horace introduced his own hollow ducks on to the surface of the water, they tipped and bobbed comically on their sides. Yet they were all ducks. The brown ones, the ones with synthetic colours on their beaks or beneath their eyes, the bright simple ones in his now-despised and abandoned little baby books with nothing but a beak and crude triangular feet for identification, and the incompetents, jostling around him in the bath-water.

The sort of bath toys that Horace wanted seemed not to exist. Amphibious landing craft and aeroplanes, submarines, patrol boats, sinking ferries with non-functioning life-rafts: Henry had pronounced them unavailable. But soap dishes would sink compellingly enough when subjected to aerial bombardment of plastic ducklings.

On some strange evenings, the bath would be hugely filled by a visitor. Lori, with her hair cleverly tied up on top, her shiny soapy breasts, her expanse of white tummy and the soft round thighs squeezing him warmly between them. Or Henry, grinning, smellier, with patches of hair in strange places, his dark wrinkled penis floating fascinatingly, heavily, on the water. Lori would push her head back between the taps, closing her eyes until prodded open by blows to her soft flesh. Don't sleep, Lori! Henry might try to read a boring, fat book while his glasses remained unclouded, but a few splashes would discourage this. Thus enlisted, they would join in the epic of the yellow ducks, the blue turtle and the red hippo. Or they would fabricate a story from the items pictured in the old plastic bath book. He knew the components by heart: a doll differentiated from a real girl by its dead eyes, a clown with four coloured balls curved over his head and his raised arms, a toy duck with wheels, a bunch of grapes, a yacht, a racing car, a mirror whose silver surface was represented by two jagged lines. If you concentrated on the mirror, you couldn't see the jagged lines; if you concentrated on the jagged lines you couldn't see the mirror. Whatever you did, you couldn't see yourself in the mirror. It wasn't that sort. It was a picture of a mirror.

Most of the time, Horace was alone in the bath while Lori or Henry drifted in or out. Among the tales Horace had been told of children who had been stolen away when they were babies or had lost themselves in the woods, there were some bath stories, of children who had fallen over into the water when nobody else was in the room and the children had never thought to get themselves up again and they had breathed in the water from the bath instead of the air and had been drowned. Other children had climbed up on the edge of the bath and fallen down and because they had banged their head on the way down they had met the same fate. Lots of things like that had happened to other children, and Horace had attempted to emulate them. How did it work? He was able to lie under the water and expel the air from inside his chest. The next step was to breathe in the water in its place, but this proved more difficult, causing nothing more than a fit of spluttery coughing.

Sometimes the bath was not there at all. Horace sat

floating with his animal friends in a giant's soup cauldron planning an escape; clinging to his raft with only a little hippo or a tortoise for food, searching for a sail which might show itself over that line where the sea meets the sky; peering down to the ground from his flying bath which was suspended under a balloon; trapped in a warm swamp with only his nose and mouth breaking the greasy surface as he moved his hands this way and that to fend off the piranha fish; steering his craft out of the earth's atmosphere and heading into deep space at warp factor one. At other times, the bath was vividly present with all its rickety, mechanical challenges. Horace would push his fingers into the crusted interior surfaces of the tap. A rotation of the pronged handle and a metallically chilly water struck his hand or foot. Flannels were there to be chewed or draped over the head and face, a blind boy cowering in his cavern with the footsteps of goblins audible in the surrounding passage. Soap was experimented with, drawn on with a fingernail, tasted with a dab of the quivering tongue, then dropped in the water where it was left to exude a white fog. As the departing water left it stranded over the plug hole, the cake of soap had decayed to a repellent, fluffy slime. Most enticing of all were the cracked tiles which just failed to join the edge of the bath to the wall. With care and concentration, these could quietly be removed while the attention of the guards was momentarily diverted. Entire mugfuls of water could then be tipped satisfyingly into the gap that had thus been revealed, with the thrill of a stream disappearing through a hole into a dark bottomless chasm. Horace never tired of the effect, and, if sufficient precautions were taken, several mugs of water could be emptied into oblivion before the vessel was fussily snatched from him. The appearance of concentration was absolute but however distant his spacecraft or galleon, he was also aware of the conversation of his parents, reunited at the end of the day, as he might have heard static on a badly tuned radio. The words were, for the most part, as incomprehensible as the wind, but like the wind they could be warm, cold, wet, comforting, alarming. Lori would have shed her business clothes, splashed water on herself from Horace's bath, rubbed it under her arms. She would lie back on the floor tugging a pair of jeans up her long, slim legs. After she had buttoned up an old check shirt, or pulled a jersey over her head and shaken her hair, she would sit on the floor, a towel in readiness on her lap. Or she might be officiously active in the bathroom or the passage outside, dispatching grubby toothbrushes, wiping circles of hardened shampoo off shelves, arranging plastic containers, purging surplus potions from the unthinkably high medicine cabinet.

'Come on, Horace, out. You'll turn into a little pink prune.'

Horace had always known that children's bedrooms were different from other sorts of rooms. The wallpaper would be decorated with rows of teddy bears, dolls or stylized versions of animals. The lampshade would be in the form of a balloon with a small basket dangling from it. Children's bedrooms had things to look at, like pointy silver stars on blue ceilings, clouds on the wall, posters of pandas and baby animals and fighter aircraft. Horace's room was not like that. It was not ready yet. The wooden stairs that linked the two floors of the flat had not yet been carpeted and were a faded brown colour, with shiny white on the edges. The man who had lived here before had taken the carpet with him for the stairs of his new house, though when he had arrived he discovered that the carpet was far too worn to re-install and didn't fit properly anyway. So he gave it to his son, for the house he rented when he was away at college, who cut one useful shape out and then threw the rest away. The steps were hard and echoey when Lori clattered down them each morning, the way the whole house had been when they first stamped around it.

They had put their old things into the flat, pictures on the wall, rugs on the floor, and the echoes had faded away. For Horace, only some of the house was his. The kitchen, maybe; definitely the bathroom. Much of the rest remained a space in which they had placed their belongings. One day his room would be painted bright yellow and red, unless he changed his mind in the meantime, but for the moment his collection perched on old green shelves in somebody else's white room. His polar bear mat, stained with a yellow and orange experiment he had once undertaken with felt-tipped pens, lay stretched across the floor, but there were plenty of bare boards speckled with spots of paint. These were satisfyingly easy to peel off with a thumbnail. A bottle top containing Horace's collection of these rubbery specks, white, light blue, and others of indeterminate colour, was perched at the far end of a shelf.

There were objects—mainly forgotten, abandoned, worn out, broken, despised—in the cupboard in the corner, but the forefront of Horace's mind was represented by the shelves which extended on either side of his bed. Nearest at hand was a megaphone with a plastic switch that could be shifted into three positions producing different sounds: the basic amplification; a metallic, robotic tone; and a more soothing, musically transformed voice. The batteries were now reduced almost to extinction, and the megaphone produced nothing but a humming crackle, whatever the setting. Most beautiful of all, safely at the back, was a cactus, standing proud out of its dry, sandy soil, contained in a laughable brown plastic pot. It was the only surviving plant in the house. Horace would caress it, feel the barbs on the pads of his fingertips. It required no care of any kind, living, it seemed, off nothing but the air of the room. Beside the inert megaphone was a red plastic bowl, removed from the kitchen, full of plastic letters backed with small magnets. A small bottle of perfume that had arrived in the mail as a free sample had been purloined by Horace, whose attention had been caught by its stopper, like a knobbly gold raisin. The bottle now pointed jaggedly to one side, resting on an anatomically incorrect rubber skeleton. New visitors to his domain were first struck by the atmosphere of medicinal incense. A carved wooden box contained gnarled, dry horse chestnuts, collected on a bounteous autumn day, their promise never fulfilled. There was a shoebox full of incomplete parts from elsewhere, half a penny whistle, the wrong half, that couldn't make any sound on its own. A three-wheeled racing car, so enticingly patterned with black stripes on red that Horace could not bear to part with it, even though its halting scraping progress on the wooden floor, a cruel reminder of what had once been, was recurrently, sweetly painful. There were unintelligible, isolated pieces of puzzle.

Most of the objects in the room were background, comfortable layers of the past. If the room had been on fire, Horace would have been torn between the bear and the Gameboy, but would probably have chosen the Gameboy and the SuperMarioland II.

Further along the countdown to bed, Horace would flap along the corridor and reach the safety of his rug and a choice of pyjamas. There was his favourite, the spruce red checks with matching buttons except for one blue corduroy button. These had supplanted the felty soft pin-striped green pyjamas whose sleeves now rode up almost to the elbows and whose shoulders gripped him as if with invisible fingers. Also acceptably natty were the navy blue, almost black pyjama bottoms coordinated with an elegant striped top, with vertical whites, yellows and blacks. The third best, the superhero pyjamas, ought really to have been the best. A Superman suit would have been something, the costume of the man who could do anything—fly and stop trains with his bare hands and never be killed by anybody. Batman would have been considerably less satisfactory, but still acceptable. With Batman, life was more complicated, and the pyjamas would not be quite enough in themselves. He needed his Bat-rope and his Bat-car and his Bat-plane. Who built them? Superman could just fly to the top of a house and rescue the girl. Batman would have to throw the Bat-hook at the end of the Bat-rope and then tie it on to something on the roof and carry the girl all the way down. No doubt these skills could be acquired, but Horace had more confidence in superpowers than in a range of appliances which had to be carried around. But at least Batman really existed. When Henry bought Horace's superhero pyjamas off a stall in a street market, he had blundered: the costume was for a fake superhero that Horace had never seen on television or in a comic, had never even heard of, a garish red strip bought because of the yellow letter H on its breast.

'Aitch for Horace,' Henry had commented, misguidedly and unhelpfully.

The initial coincidence was trivial. What did H do? What were his special powers?

'Whatever you want to do, Horace.'

The dreaded 'use of the imagination'. The ultimate sanction was Horace's, and the pyjamas were perpetually consigned to the bottom of the pile, to be used only when there was no alternative. In the previous night of accidents, the superhero costume had been tugged over his damp stiff body. Debate on the matter was generally thwarted by the toothbrush that was forced between his teeth, and as he flinched and struggled to escape, the head of the brush was jabbed this way and that, scraping his gums, prodding the back of his mouth until he retched and expelled the brush with a cough. The tooth-brushing having been fought to an honourable draw, Horace made his way to the lower of the hopeful set of two bunk-beds—they seemed to him so pointlessly bountiful—to await the next stage of the evening.

Horace's favourite things in the world apart from military hardware were sharks and dinosaurs-and-dragons, the latter combination forming a single category. There had been periods of his life when he was unable to interest himself in any form of literature which did not largely consist of pictures of one or other of these creatures, or, better still, arrangements of flaps or pop-up assemblies which made the books almost as exciting as the videos on which they could be contemplated adequately. Sharks were real, but they would never be any danger to him. There were no sharks in the chemically eye-stinging water where people swam, and sharks didn't like the noisy water by the seaside. Lori and Henry had told him so. Dragons were the safest of all. Not only did they not exist, but they never could have existed because their flappy leather wings could never have lifted such a heavy, scaly creature off the ground, and no living creature could breathe fire out of its nose; it would have burnt itself up from the inside. Think of porridge when it hasn't been blown on enough, and then imagine fire blowing through your nose. Grilled nostril, toasted tongue, charred teeth. Dragons had been made up for stories because they were the most frightening thing that could be thought, with the wings from a bat and the body from a lizard joined together, made big and given the power of fire. That was what the imagination did. That was what stories were all about. Dinosaurs didn't exist either but they once had done, long long long ago, longer than you could possibly imagine, before there had been any people. Then they had all gone, perhaps because there was no food or perhaps because something had come from space and hit the world so hard that only strong little creatures could survive. This was a pity because dinosaurs were the best of all, big and simple and straightforward. If there were teeth, they were sharp teeth. If the dinosaurs wanted protection, then there were huge bony plates all along their back. Henry had told him that when they wanted to do something, it took half an hour to do it. Like Lori, he used to say. Dinosaurs were big, and everything about them was more interesting than things that were around now. They were more interesting than sharks, but sharks were more interesting than anything that Horace actually saw in real life. The important things happened outside his house.

So Horace liked books about dinosaurs, then books about sharks, then stories that had dragons in them. Horace did not like stories that were about people like Horace, that were set in houses like his, that were about nice parents being nice to nice children playing with their brothers and sisters. What was the point of that? What he liked most of all were the stories in which gates, sand pits, wardrobes, wrong turnings, rings, carpets and pictures became gateways to other places, dangerous worlds where nothing bad could really happen. You had to get there from here, and sometimes, as Horace lay in bed wondering what he had to do to go to sleep, and the room was illuminated in slats of light from the street, he would see the toys on his shelves shift and dissolve.

3. The woman with her throat cut

HENRY FREQUENTLY FANTASIZED about the death of his wife. These were not systematic plans but rather reveries, scenarios which came unbidden in a variety of different forms. Films of possible other lives playing in his head. There would be a knock at the door late in the evening. A policeman standing on the front step, water dripping down his navy blue acrylic coat.

'Mr Dean?'

'Yes,' Henry would respond tentatively, with that heave in the stomach provoked by people in uniform. 'Is anything the matter?'

'May I come in, Sir?'

A nod and a step back. The policeman removes his cap and steps into the house with a shy bow of the head as if the doorway was too low for him, a gauche outsider unused to domesticity. Henry would lead him into the front room, where the policeman would haver: to sit or to stand? The language would be automatic. People were trained in the forms of words to be used on occasions such as these, like salesmen or people conducting surveys. If A, proceed to D; if B, proceed to E.

'Are you the husband of Mrs Lorraine Dean?'

Funny how that form of her name was never used. Or only once. At the ceremony of linkage itself, after the trembly signing in the town hall, the registrar had suavely taken the opportunity to be the first to congratulate you, Mrs Dean, as if she was the triumphant one, having snared her man by taking his name. There had been cat-calls from the direction of the bride's friends.

'Yes, I am.'

The officer would take a breath and deliver the standard lines. As designed by psychologists, or just by policemen with experience of being present at the moment when people's lives were ruined. Sensitive, sympathetic, but clear and unambiguous. The member of the public may look for reassurance of a kind which the officer cannot provide, however much he may wish to. A firm insistence on the truth is the best service that can be done for the bereaved. They must do their mourning on their own. They must go through the classic stages of grief. How many of them were there? Was it seven, or was he confusing them with the deadly sins and the dwarfs? Denial, anger, guilt, disbelief, grief, acceptance. That was only six, and Henry wasn't sure that disbelief should be in there at all. Or guilt for that matter. Lust, anger, pride, sloth, envy, gluttony. The seventh was probably mean-ness, or something like that. Happy, Bashful, Dopey, Doc, Sneezy, Grumpy. And another one. Henry and his seven miserable dwarfs. Guilty. Resentful. Sulky. Selfish. Chilly. Gloomy. And one more. Wanky. Were the stages of grief compulsory? Could you be sad before you were angry, or go through all the other stages, whatever they were, and then finish with denial and pretend it had never happened at all?

'I'm afraid I have some bad news for you, Mr Dean. I'm afraid your wife has been involved in an accident.'

Allow the bereaved to ask questions, to arrive at the truth in his own time. Establish a dialogue. Like a terrorist, a hostage taker or somebody perched on a parapet. The Stockholm Syndrome. People have a tendency to form emotional bonds with their kidnappers.

'Would you like to sit down, Sir?'

At times like this, people know the role they are supposed to play, speaking lines they've seen on TV. The pained look, sensing the worst. But you can't just say that she's dead straight away. It would look as if it was no surprise. You've got to clutch at some straws.

'Has she been hurt? Is she in hospital?'

Of course, this wasn't quite right. Henry decided that there would be two police officers, one of them probably a woman who could plausibly make sensitive, consoling faces. One police officer on the doorstep might seem like a black practical joke, the work of a maverick prankster specializing in fake deaths, allowing him to indulge in theatrical expressions of sympathy. Two is a deputation, a small group which can speak with an institutional voice. From the point of view of the police as well, it would spread the emotional flak, just as the individual members of a firing squad can divide their responsibility equally. Is it really true that one rifle in a firing squad is loaded with a blank, so that no individual can be sure that his was the decisive shot?

On their way over, the two police officers would have been giggling and gossiping about their prospects for promotion but they would have composed themselves on the step as they saw the dark shape approaching through the frosted glass. The w.p.c. would stand there with a look of concern, and the man would deliver the standard phrases which research had shown to be most emotionally effective, or perhaps just best for getting out of the house again within a few minutes and on to another job.

'I'm afraid that your wife was killed in the accident.'

No, not quite like that. Killed is the sort of word that doesn't get used by officials. But it wouldn't be a term like Passed Away; it would be something more formal-sounding, even something with a touch of the ceremonial.

'I'm sorry to have to tell you that your wife is dead.'

But that would be all. Part of the training would be to stop and allow the vacuum of a silence after the word dead. Don't gabble in order to fill it. Don't start offering confused sympathy, which may be a form of intrusion and may also allocate responsibility, which could be used as evidence in later proceedings. Don't begin to describe the circumstances in which the accident occurred. The bereaved might take some comfort in asking pedantic questions, ascertaining the precise sequence of events and cause of death, as if the details were more significant than the great non-event at their centre, the sudden absence.

Henry would sit down on the sofa, conscious of himself as the cynosure, composing his features into a suitably grave expression. It would be difficult to bear. Shift the attention somewhere else.

'What happened?'

They would tell him in guarded terms. Knowing Lori, Henry imagined the cause of death—or rather the first in the sequence of events which culminated in the fatal encounter—would be a turn to the left without indication, or the deliberate passing of a red light, or possibly both at the same time—like they do in Los Angeles, she would say, irritatingly, because Henry had never been to Los Angeles, and even if he went he would not benefit from their enlightened traffic policy because he could not drive. Lori saw an amber light as nothing less than a challenge to her ability to accelerate through a junction. The amber light was easy, almost like a green, because it was designed to allow a space between the two flows of traffic. She then realized that the first second or so of the red light was itself a notional form of amber, and even if other cars might theoretically have the right of way, how many motorists will deliberately crash in order to assert this right? She had one rule in particular: if the car in front of her could go through the lights, then she could as well. This rule was somewhere between an algebraic calculation and an adapted paradox of Zeno's in which there would always be room for just one more car, or at least always for her. To the question of what would happen if everybody did this, she would reply with a shrug of contempt at this cowardly example of the categorical imperative.

Everybody didn't. Everybody wasn't capable of doing the things that she did, and if other people attempted to emulate her, they would be less successful than she was. The other person would always blink, when it came to the moment of decision.

How long would the officers stay with him? Around half an hour. The w.p.c. would ask if there was anything she could do. A few minutes later, she would ask about children. She would give some information about a social worker or grief counsellor. Not on a printed card: that would seem too automated. People prate about needing to feel that you are not alone in your hour of need. Crap. At our moment of grief, the main thing is to feel that nobody else has ever experienced something so trying. It was difficult enough to believe in the uniqueness of nominally happy experiences. Coming out of the register office, feeling strange and alarmed—curious to see other people just walking along doing normal, daily things—and watching the next wedding party proceeding in, at the centre a young, and terribly unconcerned couple. They don't know what they're doing. Not the way that we know. Anyway, it wasn't such a big thing for us. Jackie, Lori's mother, was carrying Horace. We were just dotting the t, as Lori used to say.

There were plenty of other varieties of death to think about as well. Cancer, for example; or some other sort of terminal illness, preferably of a kind that didn't involve pain or indeed any visible symptoms beyond a slow decline. There was nothing sadistic or vengeful about these fantasies. The point was that they were focused on himself and his own responses. Sitting by Lori's bed, holding her hand, with a stoical expression on his face. Beams of sunlight through the window, poignantly suggesting a spring to come, rebirth and rejuvenation. Don't worry, I'll see that Horace grows up all right. Or perhaps she wouldn't know at all. Man-to-man discussion with the doctor. I think it would be better if she never discovered. She would probably just collapse. Let her enjoy the last months, or even weeks, that remain to her. Henry could imagine the consultant shaking his head in admiration as he left the room. My word, it makes a change to have somebody you can discuss this with properly. That woman is certainly lucky to have a man who can take responsibility for both of them, a man unafraid of death. Not like most people. And yet, which makes it even more remarkable, I suspect that he is a man who truly faces death. Perhaps he's outstared it. Somehow, I think it will be even harder for him than for her. I've learned a lot from him.

They were pleasant thoughts. Sudden accidents, violent crimes, fatal illnesses: Henry was always there helping, contemplating, stoically accepting. Rescued unconscious from the water where he had attempted to save Lori from drowning, almost at the cost of his own life. Held back from the burning house out of which he had already carried his young son. What was the highest award for a civilian? The George Cross? It is my honour to present you with this, Mr Dean. Thank you, but it won't bring my wife back, Your Majesty.

Henry gave less time to scenarios of suicide and freak

accidents. Breaking down the bathroom door and finding Lori in a red tub; a fall down stairs, or off a cliff path, bouncing improbably down the rocks. The physical details were a distraction. He was uninterested, he thought, in any form of imaginative revenge on his wife's body. It was a thought-experiment, considering an enforced change to his life. There was no pleasure in picturing himself actually seizing control of his own destiny. He forced himself to think of it now, cursorily, as a means of establishing how pleasureless it was. Sitting down with absurd seriousness and saying that it's not working and it's time we split up. Some disbelief and anger from Lori, probably some resentment because of the feeling that, if it was going to happen, she should have got in first. Then down to the timetable and the bureaucracy, the way that couples plan their holidays. Putting the flat up for sale, filling out forms, looking for somewhere cheap to live, Lori's standard of living going up, Henry's going down. Gradually telling people one by one, most of whom would be blaming him, the way people do. Custody discussions. Not pleasant to think about at all. On the other hand, there was the idea of Lori telling him. She'd do it properly: Henry, I've got something to tell you. I'm sorry—no, she wouldn't say I'm sorry. Sending out the wrong signals. I've fallen in love with somebody else. We're going to have to separate. He would be dignified. He wouldn't ask who it was. Let her be trapped with the irritation of the name on her tongue, and she'd be forced to swallow it again like phlegm, which always sticks somewhere at the back of the throat. That was more promising, a fantasy that could be saved for another busy day when there were things he should be getting on with.

The entire point of these concocted film scripts for the non-existent future was to establish Henry Dean in a state of righteous victimhood. These individualized deaths would be succeeded by the life afterwards, which would be not without its compensations. There was presumably some sort of insurance policy on the endowment mortgage, so that would automatically be paid off (though perhaps not in the case of suicide or if there was evidence of foul play: that would have to be taken into consideration) and his economic situation would suddenly become reasonably viable, even on his non-salary. Henry had heard that men were attracted to widows. An eroticism of grief. Were women attracted to widowers? He pictured the rather haughty women of his acquaintance melting under the heat of his grief and giving themselves to him, willing to do anything that might assuage his suffering briefly, offering their flesh in order to distract him from the torments of the spirit. Henry would also be arousing in his desolation: dark-eyed, gaunt, romantic and bereft. Each woman would want to be the one who symbolically restored his potency. His passive grief would function as an aphrodisiac. He thought of, well, who did he think of? Martha, Lizzie, Karen, Natalie, galvanized by his status as stoic endurer of loss. In fact, Natalie was married, and Karen had been living with Patrick, Henry's cousin, for ten years, but that wouldn't make any difference. They would still want to offer their bodies to him as a means of easing his agony, but more than that, they would be aroused by his access to authentic experience. I'm so sorry about Lori, I don't know what to do. Let me be Lori for you for just one night (one afternoon might be more exciting, as well as more practical). Let me do all the things that Lori did for you. Let me do the things Lori wouldn't do for you. Henry would think of one of them—which one this time? Lizzie—body glistening with sweat, the children all at school. Oh, Henry, make me suffer, make me suffer the way you've suffered.

Henry had never quite steeled himself to communicate this, or for that matter, any other, aspect of his imaginative life to Lori. He could imagine a frank exchange of views, a response to the question What are you thinking, Henry? going terribly wrong. You mean all these years you've been having fantasies about different ways of me dying? No, no, of course I don't mind, why should I object to my husband day-dreaming about watching me die of cancer or getting run over? Where does it come from? What is it that has put this in your mind? Henry had vague memories of stories read out to a giggling school assembly about looking at a woman with lust and committing adultery being in your heart and this adultery was just as wrong as the Real Thing, even without involving complicated lies, assignations, rented rooms, bona fide penetration and anything else you could get in a snatched couple of hours. It was just as bad to think about it, though less fun. Since it is clearly impossible not to think about adultery—well, try it, don't think about adultery—then the moral of the story was that you might as well commit adultery and get the benefits as well as the inevitable punishment.

In Henry's view at least, he and Lori had contrasting subterranean images for their conscious minds. Henry considered his brain to be a crude form of sluice-gate through which his thoughts flowed like an unimpeded river, a river operating under the sort of non-existent environmental legislation that obtained in a country like Taiwan or somewhere South American and corrupt, specifically designed to allow untrammelled economic growth. Appalling, unfiltered discharges gushed steaming out of rusty pipes from dubious factories further upstream. Transporters would arrive from distant reprocessing sites and dump irreducible waste into the fast-flowing current. Local people would tip their garbage into the river, trusting that it would at least be carried out of sight round the next bend where it would become somebody else's problem. Terrible things flowed along Henry's river: old tyres, used condoms, non-biodegradable plastic bags, cloudy spirals of noxious gaudily-coloured fluids, twists of lavatory paper, cardboard boxes, cigarette butts and other testimony to summer nights. There was nothing so disgusting or dangerous that it couldn't be tipped over the railings and lose itself with a splash in the bubbly white torrent. But nothing much sank to the bottom in Henry's stream of consciousness. If the river was drained, there would be no nasty surprises on the damp bed, no decaying messes now shapeless and unintelligible, no rusting bedsprings, rotting weed, stained plastic cartons. Just pebbles rubbed smooth, tawny sand smeared with patches of dampness.

Lori thought the imagination was more like a sewer system or, better still, a cesspit. Everything dropped in would sink and accumulate. All the turds, piss, household rubbish would decay into mush, with the flapping, slimy exceptions of the plastic containers, the polythene wrapping. Nothing was just passing through, nothing could be disowned. Everything was thrown in deliberately and it was never washed away by the tide. The image breaks down—and this was only Henry's supposition about what Lori might have thought had she been compelled to express the idea using these tools—because there would be no prospect of the individually disgusting components producing a healthy humus at the end, which could be sprinkled on the garden. If the mind was a cesspit, then it was one at high altitude or in the far north where nothing broke down and decayed, a place where the possessor was stuck with everything for ever.

Henry had once dipped his toe into the sea of revelation by telling Lori that he was fascinated by art in which women suffered, that he found this a compelling theme, pleasurable in a way, although this didn't mean that he found any enjoyment in the idea of woman suffering in real life, still less that he would want to inflict pain on a woman himself.

Henry usually hated the whole idea of getting things out in the open and talking them over, airing them, sorting them out. And as he had suspected, his thoughts and fantasies looked different when he dragged them out into the light and proffered them to Lori to finger and sniff at. They were like mushrooms which had seemed wholesome when they were being cultivated in the acrid, damp darkness of the cellar. Brought into the sunny, wholesome front room, they turned mushy. As Lori picked at them, they burst open, revealing themselves to be wormy, like the decaying flesh of corpses left unburied. What Henry tried to get across to Lori, without success, was that it wasn't just that they *looked* different in the heat and the sunlight. They *were* different. Mushrooms disintegrate in the heat. They are better off shut away in the dark of a cellar and not given too much attention.

'What about when you eat them?' Lori had responded. 'Do I have to go down into the cellar and eat them in the dark as well? That's not much use, is it? Not really something for when friends come round.'

'Now you're just arguing with the example. You've got to deal with the thing itself.'

'You're the one who keeps talking about it as something else. First it was something you throw in a river. Then it was a mushroom. If I attempt to argue with it, you say it's only a river or a mushroom and doesn't have anything to do with what you really mean.'

His insight into his own aesthetic responses came from recent visits to art galleries with Horace. They made such expeditions regularly, not because Horace had any special affinity for pictures, but because art galleries were free. You could go into the National Gallery from Orange Street and walk through it as if it were a park, looking at the colours around you, come out into Trafalgar Square and point up at Nelson.

Henry would begin an account of who Nelson was,

culled from the Ladybird *Story of Nelson*.

'He was called Horatio, a bit like you. He was a sailor, his job was fighting on boats. But he was sick every time he went to sea. No, not ill. Like me on the ferry. But there he is up there still looking at the sea.'

That was it. Henry realized that he didn't know why Nelson was supposed to be so important. Had the Battle of Trafalgar won a war? What about Napoleon? All Henry knew was stories. As they made their way up Charing Cross Road towards the bus-stop, he told Horace about the empty sleeve and the blind eye to the telescope.

Despite his regular visits and Henry's explanations, Horace did not seem to be clear about what a painting was, as distinct from a video or puppet show. On entering the National Gallery, they would weave their way on Horace's instructions towards 'the tiger'. For Horace it was not so much a picture as a process which had moved on since their last visit.

'When we saw it before, it was sitting down.'

'No, it wasn't, Horace. It can't do that. It's just a picture. It stays the same.'

'No, last time it was sitting down. Now I want to see the woman's head that's been cut off.'

It was Horace's other favourite picture.

'When we get there, you'll see that her head hasn't actually been cut off yet. They've put a blindfold round her eyes and they're about to put her head down on the block and then they'll chop it off.'

Horace's favourite sculpture, however, was in the Tate Gallery.

'I want to see the peach hanging over the banana.'

If it happened to be on display, they would search it out.

'It's not actually a peach and a banana.'

'What is it then, Henry?'

Henry looked around for a label and found it on a distant wall.

'It's called "Suspended Ball",' he said.

'Why?'

'Because that's what it is. It's a ball hanging from a cord.'

'What's the thing underneath?'

Henry contemplated the sculptured emblem of frustration, of indefinitely postponed sexual satisfaction.

'The ball wants to get down to it but it can't reach. Because it's held back by the cord.'

'Couldn't the banana climb up to the peach?'

'Maybe it doesn't want to. Or maybe it's too tired.'

'How can a banana want anything?'

'It's like in a story. Animals talk in stories, don't they?'

Horace was satisfied. Or at least he was quiet.

'One of the things about art, Lori, is that you can explore ideas without wanting to put them into practice. You can do a sculpture of the skeleton of a murdered woman made out of bronze. There's something exciting about it but that doesn't mean I want to go and cut up women.'

'Clearly I don't appreciate art properly. I know that men like doing pictures of wicked women, or of women being attacked. And I know that people enjoy looking at those pictures. And I know that women get attacked.

Perhaps those groups of people have nothing in common. I don't know. You're the one who appreciates art.'

This was true, anyway. It was with the uncomprehending Horace that Henry went to look at pictures and sculptures. It was Henry who read to Horace in the evenings, gesticulating and doing all the voices, the dwarfs, goblins, talking animals, the two of them lost together in imaginary worlds.

'Wouldn't it be great, Horace, if we could sit on this carpet and be carried off to some different world where everybody spoke English and where we'd have adventures and get back at the very moment we'd left and nobody would notice we'd been away.'

'Brilliant.'

Henry didn't believe in God, but he did sometimes wish that some superior authority, accepted by him and Lori, would listen to one of their arguments and say at the end, 'Henry is entirely correct, and Lori is being unreasonable.' If only she could be made to see that. One of their typically dysfunctional discussions had been set off by Lori commenting that he was an intrinsically unlucky person.

'And I mean that as an insult,' she had added.

For Lori believed, and repeatedly told Henry, that luck was a matter of will.

'People who believe they suffer from bad luck just allow themselves to be victims of circumstances. Bad luck is a product of ignorance, or stupidity, or incapacity. Passivity. Laziness.' These last two were accompanied by an eloquent look at her husband.

Henry could remember the setting quite clearly, late on one of those Sunday afternoons, of which there seemed to be a lot, at least in his memory: not winter, but grey with the promise of winter, an afternoon of a day during which they had not quite relaxed, not quite cleared up the house, never got around to going out for a walk or getting something done. He was sitting in an armchair drinking unearned tea surrounded by the scatterings of Sunday newspapers that he wished he hadn't read. Horace was working on a Beatrix Potter puzzle. Henry decided not to argue directly with Lori's contention. It was generally not worthwhile. Lori was adept in her disposition of artillery. The pointed general observation would, if responded to, swiftly be followed by the direct assault. When Lori commented that a person's bad luck was caused by his laziness, it was like a country launching a small experimental salvo at a border town of its neighbour, destroying a picturesque old church, perhaps even striking a school. There would be award-winning photographs of small bodies lying under sheets, and calls for retribution. But a tentative salvo in response would be crushed by a major artillery assault on a large provincial city. Any further resistance at all would be crushed by carpet bombing and a full-scale occupation—or rather, 'a temporary defensive measure to protect our interests, as is guaranteed under international law, undertaken reluctantly only because of intolerable provocation.' Better just to ignore it and find another way of attacking them. Beat them at football or question their cultural achievements.

'I don't know whether I'm lucky or not where small, everyday things are concerned, but in big things I'm sure that I'm lucky. I'm morally lucky at least,' Henry concluded with conscious provocation.

'What do you mean, morally lucky?'

Henry explained that he was lucky, for example, not to have been born in Germany around, say, 1910 or 1915.

'Then I would have been a young man when the Nazis came to power. I would have been drafted into the military services in some form or another and I would probably have been involved in some sort of atrocity or other. I wouldn't even have the excuse of being on the right side.'

'What rubbish are you going on about? Are you saying that you're some kind of Nazi?'

'It's easy for us, isn't it? We can just say how awful it all was and how dreadful it was that anybody would do it. I've got no wish that I know of to kill innocent people, or even to kill guilty people for that matter. But I suppose if it were going on, and it seemed to be all right, I suppose I would go along with it like everybody else. Perhaps I'd never get to like it, and it would be difficult at first, but I could probably get used to killing women and children, the way people did.'

Henry observed with satisfaction that Lori was shocked. Really shocked, not just wearing the expression of disapproval she assumed when she lifted a handful of dirty clothes from the floor, not huffing theatrically, as she did when loudly and ostentatiously sorting misplaced objects into piles. His wife looked not just pained, but in pain.

'That's a disgusting thing to say, even if you're just saying it for effect. In fact it's especially disgusting just for effect. Are you saying that you secretly want to commit awful crimes like that?'

'I'm not saying that I want to throw babies alive into furnaces.'

'Stop that. Don't even say it.'

'But it's all in here.'

Henry tapped the laminated exterior of a library book that was resting open on his knee. The sepia-toned photograph on its cover showed a Jewish man, eyes oddly askew, beard long and unkempt, kneeling on the ground, arms raised in surrender or in a placatory gesture. Three German soldiers stood behind him holding not the expected guns but curved canes. The middle one was grinning at the camera. There is always a clown in every group, the one who can never be persuaded to take things entirely seriously.

'I'm not talking about my own beliefs, Lori. I'm just responding to the objective evidence about how most of us behave when faced with situations of that kind. The facts seem to suggest that about ninety per cent of us will do anything, kill anybody, if it seems the unembarrassing thing to do at the time. It's not because we're threatened with torture or death. We don't want to be shown up in front of people or to cause difficulties, create a fuss. So most of us ought to feel lucky that we never have to make that choice. It's best to stay with our illusions.'

Henry was struck by another thought.

'Of course, it all depends on there not being a God. He couldn't let us get away with it all just because we were lucky enough to have been born too late. Most of us are conformists. It's just that we express it by turning up on time for work, and never get the chance to fit in with the group by meeting the norm for killing Jews. So if God wanted to be fair, he would know which of us would have committed mass murder if we'd had the opportunity and then punish us accordingly. It'll be a bit galling though. You'll be woken on the Day of Judgement, quietly confident because you devoted your entire life to caring for the differently abled. You'll walk up to Gabriel and then suddenly you'll be packed off with the goats for an eternity of being tortured. What for? you'll shriek as you're dragged down into the flames. You're a wicked Jew-killer, the Archangel will shout down after you. But I'm not, you'll howl back, I've never done a mean thing to anybody. I've never thought a wicked thought. I've spent my entire life as an enabler. Doesn't matter, he'll reply. It's just that nobody ever asked you. But you would have done. Burn in Hell, wicked woman.'

Lori applauded lightly with what Henry could only describe as a contemptuous expression.

'Brilliant, Henry, brilliant. It's so clever of you to use the murder of children to make your little debating point. And I suppose I ought to come up with a witty reference to the Black Death.'

'I don't think that that would negate my point.'

'Well, I wouldn't want to negate your point, that

would be awful, wouldn't it? How terrible to have one's point negated.'

'You're not being reasonable.'

Lori lifted the book off Henry's knee and thumbed through it. Then she tossed it back at him.

'It's two weeks overdue. Somebody's probably waiting for it. That's it, isn't it? You exist in some fascinating other world in which you can talk about maybe being a Nazi torturer and maybe not, and meanwhile I'm stuck in this tedious world in which tiresome people want library books back, and there's work to be done and things to be organized.'

She gathered up the tea things, cups, saucers and plates crammed loudly into one another.

'Do you ever feel,' asked Henry, 'that our discussions don't quite fit together in a logical sequence? Somehow, the machine doesn't perform the function it was designed for. It's as if we started doing the washing up and then we discovered that we were using the vacuum cleaner to do it, but instead of stopping and trying something else, like a dishcloth, we carry on using the vacuum cleaner and the result is that the dishes aren't properly clean, and then when we need to use the vacuum cleaner, for the carpet, well, it can't do that either because it's all full of soapy water. Do you see what I mean?'

'No, I don't know what you mean but I know what I feel, which is that I would like to take something, like this cup, for instance, and hit you over the head with it over and over again until you start thinking about your life, about our life, as if it were a real thing that needed real things doing to it in order to work better.'

'That's a terrible thing to say,' said Henry, 'especially in front of Horace. What do you think of that, Horace?'

Horace didn't reply, or show any sign of having heard.

4. The Fibonacci sequence

HENRY DEAN WAS a typical member of the post-industrial, post-managerial British economy. In 1985, when he first met Lori, he worked as a copywriter in the advertising firm Adcock, Barrell, Beard and Bloom. There used to be a tradition, of which Henry retrospectively approved, that on social occasions certain topics were taboo. These included work, money, politics and women. Each of these was a topic on which Henry had no wish to speak, and he would have liked to add to the traditional list the topics of property, acquisition of and cost; children, their sleeping practices and language acquisition, subsection under sweet things said by; crime, especially that recently committed against the narrator; London, as collection of villages; the countryside, as place to be moved to in uncertain future; schools, private, children to be transferred to; school and university, wonderful times had at; holidays, plans for. Henry had no new topics to set in their place, and on social occasions the conversation would drip from one to the other. Oh, you're a copywriter, how interesting. Didn't some novelist write the slogan, Go to work on an egg? And Salman Rushdie did one as well, didn't he? Wasn't it for whipped cream? The one that said, Be a devil. Which is ironic in a way. And they would have the famous copywriter conversation which was like the famous doctor conversation, involving William Trevor and Peter Carey instead of William Carlos Williams and W. Somerset Maugham and Sir Arthur Conan Doyle and perhaps even John Keats.

This would be succeeded by another question. Have you written anything I would have heard of? Well, have you seen the long-copy Glassafe double-glazing doublespread that ran in the professional press? That was good. Or the 10p test for duct liners? Henry had written only one slogan that had achieved any currency, in a campaign of the mid-eighties for Collini's Coffee. Research had established that coffee's notorious stimulant properties discouraged potential purchasers, even those who liked the taste and were fully persuaded of its other benefits. Henry was employed on a team commissioned to market one of the early decaffeinated brands. The slogan that resulted from weeks of work and headed the campaign, at least in its magazine format, was Henry's unaided composition: 'If you can't sleep—it's not the bean, it's the bunk.' There was no competition for authorship of the slogan because further research findings, which received extensive coverage in the specialist press, demonstrated that the campaign's effect had been precisely the opposite of what had been intended. Specimen magazine readers who were canvassed for their responses to a range of advertisements for common household products were found to have retained the impression that new decaffeinated Collini's Coffee Beans were actually designed to keep them awake at night. A further extrapolation of the figures demonstrated that, when a group who had seen Henry's—as it was by then designated—magazine advertisement was compared with a control group that hadn't, more of the second group actually purchased Collini's Coffee. The curious effect of the magazine advertisement, as one media commentator pointed out, must have been to persuade certain people who were intending to buy Collini's coffee to try something else. The failure reached a pitch of publicity where it seemed that even the firm that had perpetrated it was revelling in it. The account was quickly withdrawn from ABB&B, but by this stage, Collini's Decaffeinated Coffee Beans had become a joke in the retail as well as the advertising industry, and the product soon became nothing but an anecdote about the perils of raising a possibility, even if the intention was to dispel it. Gurus would quote it at conferences: It's like telling your potential customers, don't think about coffee keeping you awake. What are they thinking about? *Coffee keeping you awake*, the executives who had paid two hundred pounds in exchange for evangelical inspiration would shout back.

No, Henry would reply. Nothing you would have heard of. Usually just long pieces of text in business magazines. The next subject of speculation might be money. People would speculate brazenly: you must be terribly rich. Henry had never been sure what people wanted to hear. There had been a few years of relative fat, from which he had benefited with a quavering, tentative pride. But they were followed by relative decline in which the bonuses fell, and even the salaries failed to keep pace with inflation. We're the barometer of the economy, the CEO had once said to a group of them. Look at the advertising industry and you can tell what's on the other side of the hill. Henry felt like the fragile ornament sticking out at the front of an automobile, warning the rest that it was in the process of running into a brick wall. Henry's services were dispensed with due to recessionary pressure before most people knew that a recession was even in prospect. He was like the clock tower by which people set their watch. How long has the recession been going on? Do you remember when it started? Oh yes, it must have been when Henry Dean was sacked.

'Sacked' was not a word Henry liked to use, but he had, unequivocally, been sacked. One Friday morning, he had been summoned to the office of the relevant account director, Nicholas North. There was a sealed envelope with Henry's name on it, and Nicholas handed it to him and told him he was dismissed. The envelope contained his P45 and a cheque for compensation rounded up to an amount slightly more than the sum he was entitled to under his contract. There were no excuses, no explanations and no embarrassment on either side. Just the wish for this to be over and the day to begin on Nicholas's part, and a wish to kill Nicholas's wife and children slowly in front of him and then torture him to death before setting fire to the headquarters of ABB&B

its entire management was inside on Henry's. Nicholas
had read about sacking people, and so, in fact, had
Henry, in the sort of books that he browsed hopelessly
through in an attempt to discover why he wasn't getting
anything done in the office. There was always a chapter
on dismissal. *When all else has failed, the kindest thing you
can do is to make the break cleanly and quickly so that both
sides can start again.* It was crucial not to offer false hope
and not to give the impression that anything was open to
negotiation. Nicholas managed this without any ambiguity, and the meeting lasted just a couple of minutes,
long enough for a secretary to empty the contents of
Henry's desk into a black bin bag.

There is no dignified way to leave an office for the last
time carrying the tools of your trade in a bin bag while
being escorted by a security officer dressed in his slightly
pathetic sub-police uniform. Bouncers and heavies wear
dinner-jackets. Secret service men wear suits. But security
men wear uniforms, often with a supererogatory metal
label bearing the legend SECURITY on the front of their
cap. Henry was marched past an awful lot of desks,
enclaves and glass-walled offices on the way out. It was a
theatrical performance, and Henry felt himself going along
with it, even assuming the facial expressions that seemed
variously appropriate: the insouciance of a prisoner being
escorted to the scaffold, the amused indifference of a
picaresque hero heading off for new experiences, the grim
inscrutability of a man whose sufferings are too deep to be
easily communicated, each maintained in the shocked
presence of his now former colleagues, superstitiously

attempting not to catch his eye lest they somehow catch whatever he had. They had their jobs for the moment, but in a hundred years all of them would be dead, many after long and agonizing illnesses.

Henry silently wished them all bad luck as he pushed through the swing doors that led to the lift. As it turned out, the luck of those he left behind was not good, at least not in terms of their immediate career prospects. If Henry had been the first victim of a corporate balloon game, a body tipped out of the basket to keep it aloft for a little time longer, then it was too little or too late, or perhaps, as Henry later tried to explain it to Lori, it was the wrong metaphor altogether. Maybe the company was actually in a bob-sleigh race where what was needed was *more* weight, not less. Sacking Henry and those who followed him might have been like attempting to improve the performance of a soccer team by removing players. The haemorrhaging of accounts was unstaunchable, but then everybody was losing accounts. The Persephone two-in-one shampoo campaign, 'the shampoo that works as hard as you do', was considered something of a success—nobody ever told funny stories about that—but ABB&B lost the account all the same, and this was enough to sink Nicholas North's entire department, and Nicholas North along with it. He immediately got a job somewhere else—he was known to be a top talent—but somewhere less good, Henry heard.

Henry always spoke lightly of the loss of his job. He knew it was nothing to feel guilty about and he never made a pathetic pretence that he had resigned or that he had felt it was time to move on. He had been—to himself—chillingly objective about it. The industry was contracting, there would be many dismissals. And in the event, they had all been fired. The brimstone and fire had rained down equally on the just and the unjust, those whose slogans had made money for ABB&B's clients and those whose had made ABB&B an object of derision within the industry, those who were productive and those who spent most of their days on the phone or at the coffee machine, the strategists and the seatwarmers, all were victims because—it emerged later—clients had been slow paying their bills. ABB&B had been slow paying its own bills as well, and it pulled at least one graphic design company down with it.

The only really bad bit was the bit that didn't actually matter at all. After arriving home in a taxi with the bin bag, Henry had phoned Lori at school, and she had been pulled in from some playground duty, and Lori was good about it, the way she always was in a crisis: calm, practical. Henry always hoped that he would never be present at an accident and have to think about what to do while somebody was flapping about like a fish, showing bits of the body that aren't normally visible: the deep eiderdown layer of flesh, lumps of bone, improbable puddles of blood. Lori would do the right thing though, laying people down, not moving them, keeping everything all right until people who knew arrived. Mainly what Henry remembered of that day was fetching Horace from school, their walking back together, one hand enclosing his son's potato-sized bunched fist, the other holding some cardboard creation that Horace was supposed to have made all on his own. Henry didn't even think of attempting to explain to Horace what had happened. Horace had no coherent idea of his father even having a job. It was looking at Horace that afternoon that had been difficult to bear, the intense seriousness of his face as he sat drawing the giant wall of the baddies, in grey, and the tunnel that was the only way under the wall, in black, and the stream running through it, in blue.

'What's on the other side?'

'You can't see. The wall blocks it.'

Henry thought of himself as a person without illusions on the subject of fatherhood, without misplaced ideals, but he was on that afternoon suddenly and perplexingly aware of a longing to be strong for his son. This was foolish, he knew, because there was no threat of physical harm or the loss of property. The mortgage on their house was an irritation, but Lori's family had helped from the beginning. He thought of his wish to be strong for Horace in physical terms. If an avalanche swept through the first-floor window of their terraced house, he would throw himself in its path, sheltering his son. He would protect him from assault. None of this mattered, he supposed, in practice. Yet he saw his son busily crayoning, his tongue projecting from the corner of his mouth, in the shade and protection of a giant peak shielding him from wind and cold. Now Henry knew that the mountain itself, hollow and crumbling, insecure in its foundations, was no protection at all, and itself wanted to be protected, perhaps even by the small, busy figure far down on its lower slopes, lost in its shadow.

There was some embarrassment as well, even with his son, to whom the very idea was meaningless. He imagined him larger, deeper voiced, spotty, talking to friends about fathers, their money and achievements, and Horace trying to think of something that could impress his fellows and failing, and fabricating something or saying nothing.

Ever since his early twenties, with his first job, Henry had compared his financial position with other notional people of his age, mainly those he judged to be his inferiors, the people he was clearly ahead of. At first he was able to align himself quite happily with people working in the City at jobs he was never quite able to understand. He was way ahead of those who were still grimly training as lawyers or doctors, poor, hollow-eyed and ill-looking with their ninety-hour weeks. Irretrievably behind him, as it then seemed, were those who had not settled on careers, those who had headed off for years hiking through South America, or overland to India. While they were vegetating, Henry was making a career for himself. For a brief year or two in the mid-eighties, he was still mentally competing with the traders in striped shirts, staring into screens and shouting into phones. And they don't have the fun that I have, he used to think. The numbers they scream and guess about shift and evanesce each day, like clouds. Who cares which way they drift? As the second half of the eighties progressed, he was clearly being overtaken and left behind by the City group. The point, he had overheard somebody say, is to pay the school fees out of the salary and leave the bonus alone, that's the only way to keep your money nowadays. Keeping it, he gradually realized, was a term for making it increase exponentially.

His money was different from theirs. He had a small pet, a terrapin, stolidly sitting in its box and refusing to breed, while they had rabbits which were populating the landscape all the way to the horizon. Imagine a pair of rabbits breeding. Each pair produces a new pair each month which in turn becomes productive from the second month. And the rabbits are immortal. The number each month follows the sequence, 1, 1, 2, 3, 5, 8, 13, 21, 34, 55, 89 and so on, with each number being the sum of the previous two. Meanwhile, Henry's terrapin was sitting in its box nibbling lettuce and turning down all comers. Later, even the terrapin would be taken from him, while the rabbits, now in unimaginably large numbers, were still breeding.

Henry began to align himself with the clerks, with the average sort of people in suits, who had now, it seemed, caught up with him. There were plenty of exploited groups with whom he could identify—state school teachers, senior registrars, junior research fellows—but he had the queasy sensation that they were on their way up, or at least static—if only some draconian institution would impose a freeze on *his* salary—while he was drifting downwards, a disintegrating sunken ship slipping down the slopes into a bottomless sea trench. In the months after his dismissal, he assumed the role of a freelance copywriter, a market analyst, an entrepreneur, in short, and initially he earned a diminished salary, augmented by his new capacity to deduct expenses, which seemed deliriously to mean almost anything that came into his head, from his taxable income. As the work became sparser, the people with whom Henry was plausibly able to compare himself were altered once more, a few more rungs down on the ladder: hospital porters, check-out girls, librarians, shelf-stackers, pizza-deliverers, car-park attendants, lollipop men, school dinner-ladies.

Henry was now a consultant in the sense that his name remained Henry Dean. It had not been repossessed by bailiffs. No professional body had barred him from retaining it. The designation had not been torn from his uniform in front of the regiment. He had the right to term himself a consultant, just as he could have placed a sign on his door offering treatment in certain forms of fringe medicine, palm readings, astrological predictions or courses in psychotherapy. In respect of earnings, he was now, it occurred to him, at least for some of the time, off the rungs of the ladder. The ladder had kicked him away, and he had fallen off the bottom of it into space. Now he could equate himself with old lags sewing mailbags for cigarette money, runaways with shaved heads and tattoos demanding money in the street or slumped in tube stations clutching misspelt signs, senile bedridden patients drooling in long-term wards, staring duffelcoated misfits shaking their arms in the street and arguing with themselves.

There were some comforting reflections. Henry always had his education which, he had been told as a child, 'they' would never be able to take away from him. On the other hand, there was little need for them to do so, since these half-understood notions of lines and vectors, angles, architects of Italian unification, topological doughnuts, *der*, *die*, *das*, deponent verbs, map references, symbols and themes in the problem plays (Henry could remember only one sentence from his study of the problem plays: 'All Shakespeare's plays are problem plays'), *écoutez et répétez*, pipettes, Bunsen burners on flame-resistant asbestos tiles, *Omnia Gallia divisa est in tres partes*, the Eastern question, centripetal force, were in such a state of decay and disrepair that nobody could have considered it worth the taking.

Henry had other things to do. He and Lori had in earlier years employed a servant, as she was never called, whose job it was to collect Horace at lunch-time from nursery school and place him in front of the television for the rest of the day while she talked on the phone. Henry was now free to take on these duties himself. He took Horace to school each morning and at three-twenty-five he would leave the house in order to fetch Horace from school, though sometimes this would be omitted if Horace was visiting a friend. If Horace returned, Henry would superintend him as he watched television and then he would make him some supper at around five. As he performed the various duties of the late afternoon, standing by the school gate avoiding the eye of any of the other parents, opening a tin of pasta shaped like dinosaurs or spaceships in tomato sauce mixed with sausage pieces, watching Horace brandish his broomstick handle spear against the plastic sword wielded by another child, trying to think of something for them to do, rooting through stacks of video cassettes which neither he nor Horace ever replaced in their sleeves, he pondered on the phenomenon that career women and even career men talked about the pain of missing out on this.

Between the dropping off and the picking up, Henry had his working day during which he pursued his projects. I envy you your time, a friend had once said to him encouragingly. We're all of us trying to set aside time to write our books, and you're lucky enough to have it. Henry certainly had the time and he knew that all it would take would be one success, and his disabilities would seem like attractive idiosyncrasies, his previous failure a form of renunciation, even integrity. 'The collapse of the advertising agency which freed H. G. Dean to write full time now seems providential, not least for the future of British publishing, whose course has been so altered by its fruits. The human and economic results of the last recession may have been disastrous, but all those who care for the culture of the word will be unable to think of it without at least a note of gratitude.'

He had four ideas for books. None of these was for a work of fiction. Henry had always had difficulty seeing the point of made-up stories. You start a novel with a description of a character: *Sebastian Gardiner had straight blond hair which hung down across his forehead and which he would flick back with a movement of his head. His eyes were green, the most beautiful colour of all, some people think. He was not exactly handsome, the features were too uneven for that, the forehead a trifle broad, the eyebrows too pronounced, a weakness about the jaw line, but his was a face that captivated people.* Henry would be instantly paralysed, whether the writing was good or bad, whatever the difference between good and bad might be. What did it mean? Why blond, why green? There was no point in cobbling together these things that were a bit like real life, giving them a fraudulent pattern and coherence, when there was so much real experience out there waiting to be evoked and ordered. He would not be unwilling to attempt to write fiction in return for large sums of money, but even in such an unlikely event, he knew he would prove incapable of getting the words written. Why this sentence rather than that sentence? Why was this better than that? There were no stories in nature, just as there were no perfect circles or squares. Henry wanted to deal with the fractal, jagged, uneven world that was holding him back.

For his first potential literary work he already had a title: *The Brown Stuff*, or alternatively, on a more philosophical plane, *The Brown Book*: the social history, the science and the semiology of shit. The book would begin with a scientific description of exactly what shit is, what it contained, of what it consisted, why it was coloured the way it was, why it smelt so distinctively. Would it be possible, for example, for shit to smell pleasant? Perhaps our disgust at its smell is merely a culturally learned response. Or is it a philosophical idea, like arguing whether pain must be painful? This would be followed by a social history of the substance, its appearance in literature and painting and other arts, from wholesomeness to disgust and shame. Were there any cultures where people just crapped in full view without any embarrassment? India, probably, and places like that. And it used to be tipped out of windows in London hundreds of years ago. This would lead into the pathology of shit, the aversion from it and the attraction to it. Coprophagia. There were animals that eat their own shit, rabbits, Henry thought, and dogs. Investigate cats. Finally, there would be the polemical third section. A society can justly be evaluated by the way it disposes of its shit. In our shame, we in the developed world remove our shit secretly and turn it into an unusable sludge. Henry would call for a new transformative, open culture in which each household is responsible for its own shit, for turning it into a compost-like humus; a new, transubstantial, sacramental movement in which we give of ourselves back to the soil. It would be an evangelical work, eschatological and scatological at the same time, which would heal our divided self, restore us without guilt to our animal natures. While writing his proposal on this subject, Henry became excited and had a vision of a new political party, a Brown Party, which would adopt the metaphor of waste products and their recycling as its single policy. Perhaps Paradise Regained would be the best title, trumpeting the abolition of shame and disgust.

His second idea was for a travel book, based on the exotic river journeys which he had seen on TV into the heart of Africa and South-East Asia and South America. Henry had never been attracted by the idea of adventurous treks into places where you couldn't ask for things, didn't know how anything worked, were without your own furniture and possessions and where you'd drink the water and end up with worms boring into your eyeballs from the back. His own idea was for a far more modest and cheap voyage down the Fleet, the lost river of North London. He had heard vague accounts of this river which until the eighteenth, or the nineteenth, or the seventeenth, century had flowed from Hampstead Heath all the way down to the Thames. What had once been an avenue for trade and recreation, for fishing and bathing, had declined into a ditch and sewer and was gradually built over until no sign whatever of it remained. But apparently it still flowed under the streets, defiantly turning cellars green. Could you retrace its course with an extremely small boat, possibly a canoe? Or a diving-suit? There seemed something indecent about building over a river, a thing that people could stare into, that the sunlight could sparkle on. Perhaps Henry's book would be the first salvo in a campaign at the end of which all London's hidden rivers would be exhumed and returned to the city. Roads would be dug up and abandoned, and the capital would become a city of canals, rivers, railways and lanes. 'Bunyan, Blake, Cobbett, Dean, that sturdy English tradition of dissenters.'

Thirdly, he had some loosely formulated concepts for a volume about masturbation. He had been sitting at home one morning after having a wank, his groin feeling as if it had been turned half-inside-out, not like a flower opening but like a banana peel after the banana has been eaten. He was feeling the post-onanistic tristesse, so uncelebrated by the poets, wondering whether it was true that masturbation was a waste of psychic energy. Certainly he was wasting psychic energy somewhere, and this might be the explanation. Masturbation was, more obviously, a waste of time into the bargain, so tempting in advance, enthralling in the process and so pointless in retrospect. Sex with Lori was much the same of course, but then sex with Lori happened so much less frequently, and at least with masturbation he didn't have to mutter endearments afterwards. This was a book that would require delicate treatment, he realized.

The Hand Book, which was his working title, would begin, like *The Brown Stuff,* as a work of history, a hidden, subterranean narrative running under the acknowledged sexual practices. Somebody said that most of us would confess the blackest sins rather than make ourselves look ridiculous. Sex was like that. To be an adulterer, a rapist, was probably all right, assuming there was no risk of criminal proceedings. Sexual failure wasn't too bad, so long as it was in the company of somebody else. The most tawdry and unsatisfactory act of copulation would be preferable to the cheeriest of hand jobs. The book would become polemical. Masturbation is a form of sexual egalitarianism. Anybody can do it, no matter how unattractive or smelly they are. Among men all but the most terminally impotent can manage enough tumescence for what some writer had called the brief stab of pleasure. And all women, presumably, though this was where research would be needed. More than this, it was also the ultimate form of safe sex in an alienated, unhygienic age. No more shame.

You can sit there pumping away or whatever it is that women do, thinking about anything at all, and you're saving lives. Ecology of desire. That would be another good title. In a more New Agey way, *The Circle of Desire*, maybe.

The fourth and final project was another travel idea, the principal drawback of which was that it would actually require travel. The plan was a new way of circumnavigating the globe latitudinally, not at the equator but further north, a journey that would take him through many of the darkest, most miserable places of the world. Henry had never travelled any further north than the south of Scotland but he liked the sound of the countries that touched on the Arctic Circle. Separated by politics and various oceans and other natural obstacles, they were, according to some TV programme Henry had seen, or perhaps something that somebody had told him, joined by alcohol. There were alcohol belts around the globe like climatic zones. The belt around the equator was Islamic and alcohol-free. Moving upwards to the Mediterranean countries, Spain, Italy, France and so on, the main drink is wine which is drunk regularly with meals. A fair amount is consumed but people don't get drunk. Then further North are the Germanic countries, Britain, Belgium, Germany, where people drink beer, a bit with meals but also in a ritualized fashion in pubs and beer halls. Then finally in the Northern countries, pure spirit is consumed, scarcely with food at all and in a concentrated fashion in order to make the drinker fall over into the snow. The pleasure aspect has been almost eliminated, and consumption is more like an existential statement.

It all sounded good to Henry. He pictured himself beginning at Iceland, where there is so little good weather that vegetables can only be cultivated under glass or imported. Proceeding east, he would reach Lapland, which contains one of the last of the world's nomadic peoples. They follow the reindeer, except when the reindeer happen to herd into Russia. Furthermore, these are unable to live off the berries and mushrooms on which their economy has always depended because these have been contaminated by the leakage from the Chernobyl accident which drifted across Sweden in a cloud and rained down on to the last great wilderness in Western Europe.

These were Henry's kind of people, trapped in cultures of frustration. The north of Russia was just as good. He planned to travel to one of those industrial Siberian cities he had seen on TV in which people had sacrificed years of their lives to earn double the amount of roubles for their retirement. Then the rouble had become worthless and the invisible hand of the market had kept them in their purgatorial occupations without any prospect of release. Then on across thousands of miles of polluted wilderness to Canada, home of the Inuit, with their two hundred words for snow and a disintegrating culture, besieged by alcohol and Brigitte Bardot protesting about baby seals and whales. Would it be possible to eat a meal consisting entirely of whalemeat and baby seal meat? Then finally back to Iceland again.

Henry even had a title for this work, *The Ring Dove*. A

friend had told him a story about this bird, variations of which are to be found as you travel around the world, occupying small segments of the globe. As you made your way around you would notice little differences between the different kinds. Identifying them successively by letter, you would discover that A was much the same as and able to mate with B, B was much the same as and able to mate with C, C was much the same as and able to mate with D and so on through Iceland, Norway, Sweden, Russia and Canada, until you reached the point where the ring dove was meeting itself round, as it were, the other side and this ring dove, call it Z, would be quite different from and unable to mate with the ring dove A that you started out with. This would be the ruling narrative metaphor for the entire journey. Henry would be changed imperceptibly by all of the amazing experiences that he had undergone along the way, and by the time his straight progress had brought him back to his starting point, he would be a completely different person and he wouldn't recognize the Henry Dean he had left behind him. Henry didn't know if this was true about ring doves, or even if there was such a thing as a ring dove (he connected it in his mind with birds that had been ringed in order to be tracked) and he didn't want to investigate in case it wasn't. It didn't matter anyway, he thought to himself, in anticipation of later exegesis by Henry Dean scholars. It would function on the level of myth.

To express Henry's ideas in this way is to give a false idea of the process of accretion by which they had been assembled and formalized. It sometimes seemed to him that other people were not just writing books, but having them published, establishing a reputation, building up a substantial body of work, having uniform editions of their books issued, while Henry was toying with his various ideas, building them up, correcting them—one incomplete, indeed unbegun, activity, among many.

From time to time, Henry would present Lori with his ideas, for her consideration and advice. These conversations were sporadic and no more connected than the notes they used to leave each other in Horace's plastic letters on the fridge: goNe Out shoplng back 7. Theo calLed. where are you. put dinNer in herE. Henry and Lori never sat down for a good talk about it. There was no group presentation of his assembled projects, or any formality about her responses, which came piecemeal as Henry provided her with his thoughts in fragments. In sum, she was sceptical about *The Brown Stuff.*

'You're not serious,' she had said when the concept was first floated by her.

'It's an unexplored subject.'

'It's ridiculous and it's disgusting, and people won't want to read about it. And publishers won't want to publish it and I don't even want to think about it.'

'That's the whole point,' said Henry. 'It's the last taboo. People don't mind about death or blasphemy but they can't bear embarrassment.'

'That may be so, but the fact is that people will not be keen to read an entire book about shit.'

'That's a circular argument, Lori. I'm interested in doing the book just because it's a subject that repels people. I want to reclaim it as something human.'

'People will doubt your motives for doing it. It will be seen as something sick. *I* think it's sick. What this idea most suggests to me is that you should have a serious think about why it preoccupies you.'

'Don't you think the problem may be your embarrassment, Lori? Why do you find this subject so difficult to deal with?'

Henry may or may not have had a point, but it signalled the end of any further discussion about *The Brown Stuff* and the beginning of a very nasty argument which can be summed up as Henry asking Lori why she had trouble dealing with the idea of shit, and Lori countering that the more interesting question was why Henry was content to live in such a shit state which no normal person would be able to tolerate for a minute and how did he cope with the embarrassment of that?

Lori was less overtly hostile to Henry's version of a great river journey.

'The problem is that it's the exoticism of the subject that people like. I've never read a travel book and don't want to, but it's a form of fantasy, isn't it? Anybody can follow the course of the Fleet through London.'

'Anybody can't go underground in a tunnel from the Highgate Ponds all the way to the Thames,' Henry replied.

'Do you know that you can? Have you done any actual research apart from just sitting in your room dreaming about it? You seem to have the idea that there is a river running through a huge underground cavern and you'll be able to punt down it. It may just be a trickle of water dribbling through an iron pipe. That's not going to be much of a voyage, is it? I can't imagine an hour of TV inside a black pipe.'

'Even that might be interesting. The Fleet could become a river of the imagination, this abolished flood running somewhere under the city, London's suppressed subconscious still trickling underneath, emerging every so often in the form of rot or decay. A bit interesting.'

'Maybe. I can't imagine the idea stretched out for a whole book.'

'You could say that about almost anything.'

There, with what, on the spectrum of Lori's responses to Henry's pipe dreams, was relative enthusiasm, the subject of the subterranean river was left.

Henry never discussed the idea of *The Hand Book* with Lori, or even mentioned its existence. He had a bad feeling about what might ensue if she even knew that the thought of such a work had occurred to him. Years before, Lori had said to him that the important thing was that they must always be able to say anything to each other. So Henry had once asked her—once when they were lying sweatily knotted—about wanking, you know, masturbation. Lori had looked puzzled. She didn't overtly object, of course, but she wouldn't actually say the word.

'You know, quite honestly, it's something I don't understand. Who would want it if you could have real sex? And who wants it anyway? All that effort for just a little thrill. Who wants to be turned in on themselves like that?'

Henry had attempted a brief defence of the habit. He

mumbled about lonely people and then hastily improvised an argument about reclaiming control of your desire and your body which he thought might appeal to her.

'But is it something you would do, something you would ever think of doing?'

A flashing sign appeared across Henry's field of vision: POTENTIAL ACCIDENT AHEAD. REDUCE SPEED NOW. ALTER YOUR ROUTE IF POSSIBLE. Lori had to be protected from the truth. It was all right for Bluebeard's bride to open the final door and see the corpses of his former wives. That's the sort of thing you expect in a relationship. But for her to open the door and stumble in on her husband wanking over a magazine, tissues ready beside him—their relationship was not strong enough to deal with that. Lori needed to be protected from herself. Henry sensed that he would be better advised to confess to adultery, homosexuality, bestiality, anything but a casual Jodrell while she was away, or even somewhere else in the house. What I can't bear is that it's so adolescent and small-spirited, so disgusting somehow. Or perhaps she would put it with more apparent sympathy? Aren't I enough for you, in some way? Am I failing you sexually? Please tell me. I really want to know.

Lori was initially positive about *The Ring Dove* concept.

'It sounds quite interesting. The only problem . . . '

It was at this point that Henry gave an internal grimace, though his face remained impassive.

'The only problem is that it would be especially interesting if you had already done it and this had emerged from it as you went along. What you're planning to do is go on a journey in order to have an idea confirmed that you've dreamed up in your attic room from evidence that you've guessed about by watching things on TV and remembering things that people have told you or that you think you might have read somewhere.'

Lori had a particular way of smoking while she was anatomizing him that he found attractive. She gave the cigarette intelligent, staccato puffs, as if the aspect of himself under consideration were lodged somewhere between the leaves from where it had to be vacuumed out, drawn into her lungs and then exuded through her nostrils with a dragonish content. Henry could never have permitted Lori to give up smoking. It is not that he wanted her to die of a tobacco-related illness, he was sure of that. She was just so good at all the rituals and appur-tenances of the habit, all the lost crafts and folk-wisdoms, the opening of the packet, the extracting of a single cigar-ette with one hand, the snappings and clickings of the lighter, the tapping and flicking of ash. Henry had never smoked—he had suffered from asthma since he was a child—but somehow Lori smoked for both of them. She had a total conviction about her smoking, like one of those Eastern European smokers for whom considera-tions of health are a simple irrelevance. Besides, Henry came from a notoriously short-lived family in which the only traditions were diabetes and cancer and he reckoned that if Lori lost a decade of her natural existence it would probably bring her down to his level.

She took the Ring Dove idea more seriously than any

of his others. It was the only one that she thought out in practical terms. Henry attempted a defence of his strategy.

'The fact that I'm starting out with preconceptions is the whole point. I suppose that I would get back to my starting position and find that I saw it all in different terms.'

'Yes, but those different terms—so called—are part of the original scheme you started out with. That's not necessarily a problem, but being objective about it, there are a few other difficulties. Just at random, do you know how you would do this? Would you drive from Norway across Siberia? You don't know if there are roads or trains. Then somebody would have to give you a lot of money in advance to finance it, and it would all be spent just on getting around, assuming that it's possible, and then you'd have to write it and wait for it to be published and all that. And that's if you were given the money in the first place. If you're that far north and dealing with Eskimos and Lapps then it may not be a matter of trains and cars. It may be travelling with dogs, something that would take years and that you wouldn't be qualified to do however long it took or however much money you had. You've never even spent a night in a tent. What alarms me is that you've done no research at all even on the easy bits. Like this Ring Dove story. I don't know if it's true; you don't know if it's true. All you'd need to do is to find some bird book and look the bird up in the index, but you haven't even got around to doing that. And this is a plan which means trekking across Siberia and making friends with nomadic tribes. It's all in your mind, isn't it? You were never going to do this. It's a funny little fantasy that stops you arranging something you might actually be able to do.'

'But apart from that, do you think it's a good idea?'

'I love the idea. It's you that I worry about.'

'No, you don't, but it's all right. I find you very attractive when you're being contemptuous of me. I like the idea that you can be insulting me and that I can ignore your arguments entirely and just respond sexually.'

Henry began to nuzzle Lori's neck and face. He felt the soft fur of her cheek. His hand moved under her skirt against the glassy lace of her knickers, then inside the knickers and into her startling slime. Henry moved his face away slightly so that he could look Lori straight in the eyes.

'Lori, you must be excited by insulting me as well.'

'Henry, Horace is playing downstairs. Push the door shut and stop saying stupid things for the next ten minutes.'

Henry loved sex during the day with Lori. It felt unfamiliar, undutiful, almost as exciting as it would be to have sex with somebody else. And he did actually get himself organized to the point of sending out a couple of synopses and suggestions to a couple of publishers and to a television production company. He never even received a single reply, not even a piece of paper with a printed message acknowledging receipt. Henry had heard that publishers didn't even bother to read full-length manuscripts, so he wasn't too surprised.

He never began to write any of the books. He came across a reference to the Fleet, and it did seem just to be a trickle through a metal pipe. He couldn't see how he could write an entire book about masturbation without Lori discovering it and he wasn't sufficiently committed to the idea to sustain such a deception, or to pay with the psychic price of telling her about it, and that was all before the effort of the literary work itself. The shit book and *The Ring Dove*, though, he still kept hold of, without violating their purity by actually finding out new information on the subjects. In practice, they would never have measured up to the idea of them that he had in his head.

5. Turn me on, Dead Man

'WHICH ONE IS it? Why can't you ever write the names on the labels?'

Horace was sensitive to noise and put his hands over his ears. Lori was in the kitchen, and Henry had shouted, though the kitchen was the next room, and there was no need. Lori replied without even troubling to raise her voice.

'Which one is what? Anyway, we only have about four videos that aren't cartoons. It can't be hard to find. I'm sorry I can't deal with that at the moment, I'm out here clearing up. If you come and take over, I could try and find it.'

Henry ignored this. Lori was emptying the washing-machine. Horace was sitting at the table writing his diary in two colours: black and red. Henry was on his hands and knees, poking behind the video recorder, feeling for the fugitive tapes. He began to sing softly, so that Lori wouldn't be able to hear.

'Mum was in the kitchen hanging out some clothes, When down came a bla-ackbird . . . '

'Don't say that,' said Horace.

'It's only a song.'

'How do you spell video?'

'V-i-d . . . er . . . e-o. But I haven't found it yet. You can't write about it until we've watched it.'

'I'm writing that we're *going* to watch it. I'm writing things we're going to do in red,' said Horace.

'That's not very interesting, is it? Diaries are for writing what actually happened. Or maybe what you wanted to happen.' Henry pulled himself out from behind the television clutching a small stack of tapes. 'When you're grown up and reading your old diary, you're not going to care very much that you were *going* to see a video of *Where Eagles Dare*.'

'Oh, Christ, you're not going to watch that again, are you? You've seen it about ten times.'

Henry twisted round. He was suffering from a minor, unidentified ailment of the lower back, and he had to rotate his entire torso. Lori was standing in the doorway, sleeves rolled up, washing-up gloves provocatively in place.

'I know, I know. But it happens to be about the only film I really like, and it's time that Horace saw it.'

'I thought Theo was coming.'

'He is. He is. He's going to watch it with us. Is there a problem?'

'I don't mind. He's not *my* friend. You're just going to sit next to each other and watch a war film.' She turned to go. 'Don't men ever want to talk to each other?'

'I haven't got anything more to say to Theo. I said it all at school.' Lori was gone and Henry was muttering to himself. 'What are these names? I've never seen any of these.'

Henry pressed a button, green glowing numbers surfaced on the dark plastic fascia. He pushed the cassette marked ORESTEIA into the machine's maw, and it gave a clattering gulp and swallowed. He pressed a number on the handset.

'The video channel is on five, isn't it?

'It's on twenty-six.'

'Why?'

'I don't know and I don't know how to change it.'

Henry pressed two stroke and six. A football match appeared on screen. Henry hated football. Lori had no interest in sport of any kind. He could think of no reason why they should have a football match on tape. He pressed the eject button and inserted the cassette marked MAHABARRRRBRBEBARATA. Three men were having a political argument. This must have been an old recording, because Henry remembered that one of them was dead. He pressed fast forward. Once, it had seemed funny to speed film up, but it wasn't any more, now that everybody could do it. It went on and on. He switched off and pressed the *really* fast forward. Dumdedumdedum. Empty space. How much of life consisted of null little episodes like this? Henry imagined himself one second away from death and permanent extinction, remembering moments of this kind. What a waste they would then seem. Except for the ones when he had been thinking thoughts like this about them, of course. He pressed play again. The argument was still continuing. He ejected the tape and exchanged it for one marked THE SACRIFICE. A car hit a snowdrift. A German soldier flew through the window. Good. He switched off and pressed the rewind button. Lori was in the room again.

'I wish you'd told me you were going to watch a video. I would have arranged something.'

'How do you spell bottom?' asked Horace.

'You could watch it with us. B-O-T-T-O-M. He's about my only friend. I don't see why you have to be so bad-tempered every time he comes over. And he's Horace's godfather, you ought to remember that.'

The instant that Henry said the word 'godfather', he knew that he had made a mistake. He had got carried away. Before that, he had been ahead. Lori had got cross about the evening a little bit too quickly, without suffi-cient provocation. The talk of Theo as Henry's only friend was good. It was very good. It introduced the note of pathos and self-pity. But the mention of godfather-hood was bad.

'I don't think I want to talk very much about Theo as Horace's godfather, if that's all right with you.'

'We've talked about all this, Lori. It's obvious that Theo couldn't really deal with the idea of that. It was my fault for asking him.'

'Oh, crap. It's nothing to deal with. All he needed to do was to buy a book of fairy tales or something and write his name on a blank page somewhere near the beginning. The man is a fucking oaf.'

There were various things that Henry didn't point out, because they were the sort of things he had pointed out before, with disastrous results. The first was that when Lori said she didn't want to talk about something, the two of them always ended up having a row about that very issue. The second was that he had never wanted Horace to have godfathers and godmothers, and that it was Lori who had said it would be a nice gesture to ask Theo. He had been asked, and nothing had ever been heard of it again. No present. Nothing said. They had wondered whether Theo had forgotten or not taken it in, and then time passed and it was never mentioned, except by Lori, grimly, whenever Theo's name came up.

'Lori, could I just say that one, he's the only person I could remotely refer to as a friend, and, two, Horace is now seven, and it's a long time ago, and, three, Horace, why do you want to spell bottom?'

'I'm writing about my dream.'

'What dream?'

There was a ring at the door.

'I had a dream.'

'Aren't you going to answer the door?' said Lori.

'I want to hear about this dream.'

'I dreamt that somebody was putting paper into my bottom.'

'What do you mean?' said Henry. 'What did you have a dream like that for? Who was doing it?'

Horace had resumed his writing and was no longer paying attention. Henry had moved towards the hallway but he stopped.

'Well, don't tell anybody about it.' There was no response. 'Hello, Horace, I'm here, this is your father speaking.' He cupped his hands around his mouth. 'Hello, come in, Horace, are you receiving me? Please acknowledge. Could you say something, or make some sign, to show that you're listening? Is the boy autistic? Has he had a stroke? Could somebody hold a mirror in front of his lips?'

Horace looked up.

'I heard what you said.'

'What do you think, Lori? I wonder if we could rub it out, or perhaps you should rip the whole page out.'

'For Chrissake, Henry, what are you going on about? It's only a dream.'

'Tell that to your mother. She'll have me sectioned. They've probably got some fucking My Dream thing at school and Henry will be talking about how things were being put into his bottom. The next thing we know, he'll be in care and I'll be being gangbanged in a remand cell.'

'Now, I wonder where Horace's dreams might be coming from. Are you going to let your friend in?'

Theo was wearing a shiny grey suit, shiny in a way that left Henry worried about whether it was inordinately cheap or inordinately expensive. As soon as he was inside the house, he removed his brightly coloured tie—there was a flash of an exotically plumed bird before it was crumpled and crammed into the pocket of the raincoat folded over Theo's arm. To Henry, Theo always looked as if he was playing at wearing a suit, perhaps because they

97

had known each other since primary school, but the impression was reinforced on this occasion because Theo was carrying his attaché case under his arm instead of by the handle. Like Henry, he was only in his mid-thirties, but he had the heavy, baggy jowls of a middle-aged man, burdened with commitments. His wiry, dark curls were plastered against his head by the rain—perhaps he had been using his case as an improvised umbrella—but he looked much the same as usual because he was given to sweating copiously. His suit had clearly been assaulted by moisture from without and within, speckled on the shoulders, dark under the arms. He nodded at Henry and walked straight through into the living-room.

'Lori.'

'Theo. Hard day at work?'

He sat down heavily on the sofa. Too comfortably, Lori thought. Immovably. He opened his case and took out a bottle wrapped in brown paper. Whisky.

'Have you got some glasses? I've not been at work. I'm on a retraining course.'

'Oh dear, not been selling enough pensions?'

'We've been selling too many. It's a sort of legally required training course.'

'I see,' said Lori. 'Like having to retake your driving test after driving while drunk and killing a child?'

'That's not a very good comparison, Lori. We weren't drunk. We were trained to kill children. Now they're training us not to. Hello Horace, what are you up to?'

'He's just writing something,' said Henry, lifting Horace's notebook and placing it on a shelf. 'But he's stopping now because we're going to watch *Where Eagles Dare*.'

'Great.'

'Haven't you seen it?'

'No, only a few times. And not for ages. Anyway, I don't properly understand it yet. Shall I go and get a take-away or something?'

'Let's get the film going, it lasts about two-and-a-half hours, and then we can talk about food while it's going on. There we are. Is that it? Yes. Come on, Horace, get into a position where you can see properly. Doobedoo-bedoo. Doobedoobedoo.'

'That's a German plane.'

'That's right, Horace. But it's only pretending to be German. You see, they're in German uniform but they're really British soldiers. Except that that one's American.'

'Are they goodies?'

'Yes. Except that some of them are baddies pretending to be goodies.'

'Which ones?'

'You'll see. You're not meant to know.'

They pushed the sofa round in front of the screen. Horace sat in the middle with Theo and Henry on either side. Lori moved around the room picking up newspapers, cups, a half-completed puzzle. She went out of the room. She returned with a book and her cigarettes and perched on the arm of the sofa. Henry asked if there was any food for supper. With a snap of her lighter Lori replied that there was if Henry had bought any. And cooked it. Theo suggested again that he order a take-away. Henry asked if they had any menus from local places. Lori replied that they must be wherever he put them, since she never ordered take-aways. Henry found them in the hall.

'There's Chinese, Indian, pizzas, Malaysian, carpet cleaners, taxis to Heathrow and some junk mail for the people who lived here before. No, that bit's before. They're explaining what the mission is. What the goodies have got to do.'

Theo thought he was allergic to Chinese food. Lori didn't like pizzas. None of them knew what Malaysian was really like. So Indian it was. Horace's frowning gaze remained fixed on the screen.

'Who's she?'

'She's the friend of the head goodie.'

'Which is the one with aubergine in? You know that Richard Burton used to drink three bottles of vodka a day. I mean, look at him, he's completely arseholed. And he's meant to be fucking that woman and jumping between cable-cars.'

'For Chrissake, Theo,' said Lori, gesturing towards Horace.

'It's OK,' mouthed Theo almost silently, 'he won't understand. Anyway,' resumed his normal tone, 'he's so gorgeous, perhaps women didn't expect much in the way of performance. Just doing it with Richard Burton was enough. What do you think, Lori? Is he your type?'

'No, Lori likes a rougher sort than that. Stubble and greasy hair. Like that one, what was he called? The one with the greasy hair who drives around on motor bikes and became a boxer. Untamed. Unwashed really, as well.

Isn't that true, Lori?'

'Now that you're actually having a conversation and you're explaining my sexual preferences, would you like me to put Horace to bed?'

'I don't want to go to bed. You promised. What's he doing now?'

'He's calling back to base. Back to the goodies. Or the sort of goodies.'

Henry went to phone for the food.

'Listen, Horace,' said Theo, 'have you heard my Richard Burton impersonation? It's brilliant. Listen: Bro-o-rd S-o-o-rd c-a-a-lling Danny B-o-o-y. Bro-o-rd S-o-ord c-a-alling Danny B-o-o-y.'

Horace began to giggle, his entire body vibrating like a primitive generator that had juddered into motion. He fell into the space that had just been occupied by Henry and then on to the carpet. Henry returned from the phone.

'You look wonderful in your suit, Theo. That's the only thing I really miss. I used to like dressing up every morning. I should show you some photos of my dad when I was little. He must have been in his twenties but he used to wear a suit and tie to go to the beach. I dress like Horace nowadays.'

The food was mainly finished, except for some cold remnants of sauce stuck in the corners of the foil. The allied force was now inside the Schloss. The last of the whisky was in Lori's untouched glass. Theo looked at it several times and then drained it. He looked at Lori's overflowing ashtray with some awe.

'You know, you're an amazing smoker, Lori.'

'It's great, though, isn't it?' said Henry. 'That's why she's got that wonderful croaky voice, for one thing. It's worth smoking just for that on its own. Do you remember that TV commercial attacking cigarettes? Kissing her is like kissing an old ashtray. Crap. It's like sticking your tongue into some slightly burnt, but still runny meat.'

'Shut it, Henry.'

'What is he saying?' asked Horace.

'You tell me,' said Theo. 'I'm completely lost.'

'No, it's not that complicated,' said Henry, 'you just have to concentrate. Those three were pretending to be English pretending to be Germans, but really they were Germans pretending to be English. Pretending to be Germans. That's easy. The hard bit is that Smith, the leader, is English pretending to be a German pretending to be an English pretending to be a German.'

'Why?'

'He's actually Welsh,' said Theo. 'In real life. Was. In fact, in real life he's actually dead.'

'What about him, is he dead?' asked Horace.

'He certainly is,' said Henry. 'Shot right through the head.'

'Do you think it's right for Horace to watch things like this?' asked Lori.

'It's all right, Horace,' said Henry. 'It's all just pretend. He's not really dead. It's like a game.'

'I knew that,' said Horace. 'You didn't have to tell me.'

'If you think this is bad, you wait for the cable-car

fight when Peter Barkworth gets the ice-pick in his arm, and the other one gets kicked in the face and falls off. That's the really good bit.'

'All right, that's it, Horace, time for bed.'

'I don't want to go to bed. I want to see the end.'

Henry stepped in, disastrously.

'Lori, you have been negative about every single thing that has been said or done this evening. If you hate the film so much, then why are you watching it? Haven't you got some ironing to do or something?'

Even Henry was surprised. Somehow, the joke didn't sound funny in quite the way it had when he launched it down the chute. He had pressed the button marked Ironic Comment, and that had come out. Without a word, Lori raised herself from the arm of the sofa and left the room. One of the interior layers of skin in Henry's face seemed to have raised its temperature. He caught Theo's eye and made various pantomimic gestures, a raise of the eyebrows, a mock grimace, he pointed his fingers at his head as if they were a gun.

'Do you want me to go and talk to her?' asked Theo.

'What about? I don't think you understand the niceties of the situation.'

'Is that a machine-gun?' asked Horace.

'Yes, but they'll get it with a grenade.'

'Brilliant,' said Horace.

Theo gave a theatrical look into his empty glass.

'Have you got any whisky? We seem to be out.'

Henry fetched a bottle from the kitchen. Lori wasn't there.

'Do you want more water with it?'

'Don't worry. The point of the film, Horace, is that you've got to be careful who you trust. The only way that Smith could be sure of anybody was when they had been murdered. And he could only trust Clint Eastwood because he didn't know him at all.'

'And the woman because he was in love with her,' said Henry.

'And the woman because he was in love with her,' said Theo. 'And that's why your father is such a lucky man. You see, that's what life is really like. You just don't know who to trust, who may be a spy in disguise. There are lots of examples. Like Paul McCartney.'

'Who's he?'

'He was this very famous man who wrote wonderful songs and in 1968 he died and his place was taken by someone pretending to be Paul McCartney who couldn't write good songs.'

'Theo. We've got a rule in this house about gross stupidity. Subsection, limitations thereunto.'

'Don't worry, Henry, he's not listening. Anyway, small children don't take these sort of things in.'

The whisky finished, Theo fell asleep, and Horace sat in Henry's lap for the final sections of the film.

'Do you remember when we went on a cable-car?' Henry asked. 'But you couldn't get out of a cable-car in real life. And you wouldn't be able to jump from one to the other.'

He kept expecting Horace to drift into sleep and

occasionally peered round to look at his face, but the frown of concentration remained constant.

'Where are those bombs from?'

'Those are the ones they set earlier in the film, before they went up to the castle, do you remember? After the German flew through the window and they pushed the car over the side of the cliff.'

Clint Eastwood reached over to shut the door.

'Where has the man gone?'

'He jumped out of the plane. He was the chief baddie. They've done it all now. They've found out all the baddies who were pretending to be goodies. They've got the list of all the German spies in England. And they've killed almost all the soldiers in the German army. And they've escaped completely unhurt.'

'No. He got shot in his hand.'

'That's right, Horace, but it's not too bad.'

Horace sat up.

'Mission accomplished,' he said.

Henry made a half-hearted attempt to persuade Theo to stay the night, but it was while he was waiting for the taxi company to answer the phone, so it wasn't convincing. Theo sat on the sofa, dazed and chastened.

'I missed the cable-car fight. What did you think, Horace? Something for your diary.'

'Brilliant. It was brilliant.'

'I wish I'd fought in the war.'

'Oh for God's sake, Theo.'

'No, I do, really. Have you seen *The Dambusters*? Let's watch that, next time. Lori would like it. There are even fewer women than there are in this film. Except for the inventor's wife. What's the time now? If we'd been in the dambusters squadron we'd probably be getting ready to set off at about this time. I'd have my flying jacket on and I'd be having a last cigarette out on the tarmac. It's still so dark that you can hardly see the Lancasters scattered out across the airfield, just a few silhouettes against the sky where the dawn will be in an hour or so. The airfield would be busy, but you'd think about how out there, across the fields of England, people were asleep in their beds. Funny really. There I'd be, in the heart of English countryside, in the Cotswolds maybe, or in Kent, the first bird of the day starting to sing. Then I'd climb into the rickety giant, nod at my co-pilot and prepare to head out over Germany. I'd make a last attempt to listen to that bird. Then Contact. The engines would start.'

There was a knock at the door.

'That's your cab. A pity. I was curious to hear what happened on the mission.'

'I get back, of course. It's breakfast time and I go into the mess where they're serving bacon and eggs—some more women in the film there, serving the breakfast—and I see the empty spaces. But we don't talk about them.'

'Those are the ones I always identify with. That would be me. Failed to return. I'd be the one whose bouncing bomb missed the dam altogether and blew up his air-craft.'

'You know, Henry,' said Theo as they walked down

the stairs to the front door, 'men who have been in action together must share something that is more intense than any other kind of experience. It's like when we were on stage together in *The Boyfriend*, remember the way we depended on each other?'

'All I remember is feeling sick for every second of it. Sick when I was getting ready to go on stage, then sicker when I was actually out there, then a bit less sick when I came off. Then I drank half a bottle of Bacardi and I really was sick. I don't think there was very much that was special about it.'

Theo paused in front of the open door of the cab.

'Raincoat. Case. Bottle of whisky. Drunk. Me. Drunk. What have I been talking about?'

'About wishing you'd fought in the war.'

'Before that.'

'You talked about Paul McCartney being dead.'

'God, I'm sorry. It's all meant to be in that Number Nine Number Nine bit when you play it backwards. I once tried it but my record player won't work backwards. Do you know who I would really like to fuck?'

Theo paused, apparently expecting an answer.

'No, I don't.'

'Well, guess then.'

'Someone you know? Geena?'

'Vanessa Bell.'

'Who?'

'Go south,' said Theo to the cab driver, whose response was inaudible. 'Well, towards the river Thames. That way.' Theo pointed down the street.

'Except she'd be about a hundred now. If she were alive.'

The cab moved away while Theo was talking, and Henry heard something about pension salesmen but he had no time to reply.

With no story, but a few questions about the German army, Horace was in bed and quickly asleep. Henry went into the grown-up bedroom. The light was on, but there was no sign of Lori except for a ridge of duvet on the far side of the bed.

'Are you awake?'

There was no sound or movement. Henry forced his training shoes off without undoing the laces. He lifted his sweater and T-shirt over his head together and likewise took off his trousers and knickers together. With his socks, they were all tossed on the wicker chair in the corner. The sight of the bulging bed administered a prick to his conscience, and he returned to his clothes, retrieving the socks, pulling the T-shirt out of the sweater, the knickers out of the jeans and placing them in the plastic clothes basket on top of Lori's knickers, socks, trousers and shirt. Henry got into the bed and switched the light off. Lori was lying with her back to him. He placed the long middle finger of his right hand into his mouth and very gently sucked and moistened it, not with his tongue but with the inner surfaces of his mouth so that it became slimy. His left hand eased one cheek of Lori's buttocks away from the other, then he inserted his slippery finger into her anus. There was some initial resistance, but it yielded, and the

THE DREAMER OF DREAMS

finger entered up to the first joint. For a moment, it was gripped tightly and warmly. Henry could feel a pulse. He was getting away with it. Greatly daring, he pushed it in right up to the knuckle. Then he heard a sharp cry and felt a fist strike his nose.

'You stupid fucking idiot, what do you think you're doing?'

'I was wondering if it would be possible for you to have sex when you were asleep. Would it be physically possible for you to come?'

'Well, it didn't work, did it?'

'That wasn't the real experiment. I was just fidgeting, really. You weren't deeply enough asleep. But if you were in the middle of a dream it might feel like real sex. This might be a way of freeing yourself to do the things that you don't normally want to do.'

Lori turned and raised herself on her elbows.

'Henry, I don't want to be freed to do the things I don't want to do. I don't want to do them.'

Henry snuggled up against her.

'You're just inhibited, Lori. I'm surprised that you can't see that there's a pleasure in allowing yourself to be forced to do things that you think you don't want to do.'

There was a grunting, huffing sound of disagreement from the darkness.

'Perhaps I can try this experiment as well,' Lori replied. 'When you're in deep sleep, I could come and put the dustpan and brush in your hand, or the ironing, or guide you downstairs to the washing-machine. Or I could sit you down at your desk with some job application forms.'

There was a long silence. Henry was assessing the injury to his nose, now that the spiralling pain had faded. He pushed his finger into each nostril in turn and then tasted it. No apparent blood.

'I apologize for what I said about the ironing.'

'That's all right. Did you enjoy the rest of the film?'

'I think Theo's got a new girlfriend. Or he's going to have.'

'I don't envy her.'

Henry nuzzled up against Lori.

'We ought to have sex after we've argued.'

'That wasn't an argument. Anyway, I don't want to have sex tonight.'

Henry separated himself from her.

'Well, I do. I'll just have a wank then.'

The bed began to chug gently, as if it were a canal barge with a barely adequate outboard motor.

'All right, all right,' said Lori.

Henry turned and put his arms round her.

'No, stop that. I mean that I'll toss you off.'

She pushed Henry on to his back.

'There now. You can imagine it's a prostitute doing it.'

'I could never fantasize about anyone except you, my love.'

6. Which woman is his love greater than he told that it was?

'WHY ARE YOU here?'
   'Because my doctor sent me.'
   'That's not a proper answer.'

Henry's doctor refused to believe he was ever really ill. Dr Inglis was an unhealthy-looking, florid-complexioned, broad-girthed woman. She was robustly medieval in appearance and had always been unwilling to write prescriptions of any sort for Henry. She had a nice cop/nasty cop manner, either pooh-poohing the idea of any treatment at all, or else sending Henry off to a hospital specialist for the most trivial muscle strain. The method worked, and Henry stopped coming to see her at all, though he sometimes wondered whether her actions might have been different if she had been paid like a dentist, according to what was done, rather than as a doctor, according to the number of patients on the books. Above all, whatever the symptoms, she tried to persuade him to go into psychotherapy.

'Everybody should have psychotherapy,' she had once said, when Henry was in her surgery complaining of a stomach pain.

'I just want you to give me something to make it go away. A pill, or some kind of liquid.'

'It would be easy for me simply to give you something like that. Most doctors would just write you out a prescription.'

'That's good enough for me.'

'But you oughtn't to be getting illnesses like this. We need to ask why it's happening.'

'I know why it's happening. I'm worried about my life, there's no mystery about it.'

'Practical matters of that kind oughtn't to be making you ill. You shouldn't be worrying in that way. That's exactly what we should be dealing with.'

'I'm worried about my life because my life is worrying. And my stomach is hurting. I have to do things. To sort out my life. Which is hard, and I will have to do them on my own. And I can remove the pain from my stomach, which is what I've come to see you about.'

'I want to stop you worrying.'

'Thank you, that's nice of you, but it's about as useful as telling a man who has jumped off a high building that you want to stop him falling. He will stop falling when he hits the ground.'

No, that wasn't quite the right example. Somebody falling could be helped by being caught. Henry would have liked a doctor who could give him avuncular advice, or someone young with whom he could chat on equal terms. Instead he was trapped with this holistic troll who seemed not to believe in western medicine.

'One comparison I tried to explain to Dr Inglis, and this is part of my problem with talking to you, is that of somebody lying in bed with a hole in the ceiling above, and water is dripping through on to them. Now, in the short term, you want to get out of the way of the water and perhaps put a bucket or something there. In the long term, you want to get the roof fixed. Dr Inglis's response was to wonder why I was worrying about getting wet. She would arrange for me to have psychotherapy in order to rid me of this neurosis. Then I would never have to get the roof fixed at all, or even get out of bed. Except to go to therapy.'

'You like using examples. Do you have difficulty dealing with things as they are?'

Henry had, in fact, been trying to obtain Prozac. He had read about this new pill in a newspaper or a magazine somewhere. It was one of many drugs for treating symptoms of depression, and that was fine. However, claims were made on its behalf that went far beyond the mere alleviation of gloom. The pill's advocates claimed that it had the capacity to alter the personality for the better. The shy person would become confident, thwarted creativity would be unleashed, the pessimist would become rapturously hopeful. This sounded about right, a chemical that would change not Henry's attitude but Henry himself. Instead of sitting in his house pretending to be Lori's husband, pretending to be Horace's father, pretending to be leading a busy and effective life, he would be able properly to assume those roles for the first time. They would no longer even be roles. He would *become* those things. He went to see Dr Inglis.

'No, no, no, no, no.'

'Are you trying to say that you're against the idea?'

'Henry, what do you want? I'm not going to give you some pill to try to make your life better.'

This time, Henry was determined.

'I'm sorry, Doctor. I've done research on this. I've got the classic symptoms that this pill was designed to treat. I'm feeling miserable, I'm sleeping badly, I've lost weight. I'm suffering from depression that is interfering with my capacity to do my job and with my home life. It's clearly the right thing for me. If you won't prescribe it for me, then I'll change doctors and find somebody who will. I need this pill. I have to have it. If I don't get it, well, you may be held responsible for something happening to me.'

Dr Inglis thought for a long time, frowning like an ogre from a pantomime. She bounced the eraser-end of her pencil on the desk, as if she were thinking in Morse. OK chaps, scramble. Bandits over Biggin Hill. Is your kite all right, Henry? Bit shot up, Sir, but she'll fly. Good man. Tally ho, then. Yes, Sir. Don't wind your clock. Don't leave a letter to be posted later. People who do that don't get back.

'I'll make a deal with you, Henry.'

'What do you mean?'

'You go for a trial session with a psychotherapist. As you know, I think a course of therapy will be far better for you than any pills. But if you don't like it, then I'll prescribe some form of fluoxetine for you.'

'The pills don't cost thirty pounds a week, and you don't have to travel across London to take them.'

'Why should everything be easy? Will you accept my challenge?'

'All right.'

'I'm going to send you to a woman called Natasha Kaposi.'

'Like the sarcoma.'

'You'll like her. All the men I send to her fall in love with her.'

'I thought everybody fell in love with their therapists. I thought that was the whole point. You mean really fall in love with her? I suppose if I left my wife and child for her, that would be one way of solving my problems.'

'You won't be able to resist her.'

Natasha Kaposi lived in a flat in a house in Ladbroke Grove of the sort that seemed far too large for any family ever to have lived in, even with all the governesses and retainers and gardeners. Her flat, though, was small, like one of the bits of space that had been left over after the multiple conversion some time back in the eighties. They started converting from the attic downwards and from the cellar upwards and then found themselves with an irregular polyhedron in the middle, all sloped ceilings under staircases and multiple corners, two rooms smaller than the hallway between them. She was a woman of young middle age, dark with olive skin, Henry thought at first, but then weren't olives green or black? There were no olives with richly light brown skin. Perhaps the expression implied that the person's family originated from a place where olives grew. That looked about right. Her surname sounded Italian. She gave no smile when she let Henry into her flat on the third floor. She was dressed with studied anonymity. Flat shoes. Dark trousers that weren't jeans. A black, unpatterned sweater. No jewellery except for the sort of ethnicky earrings that all women wore.

'Dr Kaposi, I presume.'

'I'm not a doctor,' she said. 'Come through here.'

She gestured Henry into a small room containing, he was almost embarrassed to see, a genuine couch. There were no pictures on the walls and no other items of furniture except for an armchair, slightly behind the head of the couch, close to the door. Almost everybody becomes obsessed with their analyst. They become curious about every detail of her life, any little titbit that they can infer about her existence outside the analysis. Patients want to fuck their analyst. Sometimes they do fuck them. Henry imagined fucking Natasha Kaposi on her couch. How many people had lain on that couch imagining sex with her? Perhaps she had had sex with some of them.

'Do I have to lie down on this?'

'It's probably best, but do what you feel comfortable with.'

Henry lay down, feeling cross and rebellious. What

did she mean by 'feel comfortable with'? Even by choosing whether to sit or to lie down he would be signalling that he accepted the situation they were in and her control over it. He was not going to be embarrassed. He was not going to be evasive.

'Before we start, could you tell me how much this costs?'

'Each session costs thirty-five pounds, payable in advance, and lasts for fifty minutes. This introductory session is an exception. You may pay me afterwards. After this, we decide how our sessions will operate. You must also pay for sessions you miss, which includes any holidays apart from those I take during August and over Christmas.'

'Yes, I've heard about that. The payment of the fee is a symbol of the patient's commitment to the therapy. And it's good for cash flow. At the company I used to work for, we used to try and convince our clients of something similar. They'd show their commitment by paying on time, and we'd show ours by doing good advertising. Our system didn't work, and yours does. That's why you're sitting there and I'm lying here. What do you want me to say to you?'

'That's up to you. You can say anything you like.'

Henry found it easy and pleasant to talk and saw no reason not to be frank about the deal with Dr Inglis that had brought him to this couch.

'She said I'd fall in love with you,' he concluded. 'She said that all her male patients fall in love with you.'

It was unsatisfactory for Henry that he was unable to see the effect of his words on her. There was a pause.

Henry was not used to allowing silences in conversation but he forced himself not to speak.

'I suppose that Dr Inglis was joking,' she said. 'In any case, what she said was in confidence between the two of you. Why have you told me?'

'Why shouldn't I? I thought anything was allowed in analysis.'

'But why should you?'

'You're the doctor.'

'There are many possible reasons. To embarrass her, or to embarrass me. To impress me or—how would you say?—to rattle me. Perhaps to establish a complicity between us against your doctor. To flirt. To demonstrate a lack of inhibition. To evade. Why have you resisted treatment of this kind?'

'Don't mistake me . . . sorry, what should I call you?'

'Call me Natasha.'

'All right, Natasha, don't mistake me. I'd be a terrific therapee or whatever they're called. I don't think I'm particularly plagued with complacent illusions about my life, though. I don't especially have resentments against my wife. Just a few normal ones. I mean, how does she know she doesn't like sodomy unless she tries it?'

There was no reaction.

'I love her and she probably doesn't love me any more, or at least she has reason not to. I'm failing in a public sense, meaning that I don't have a job, or any prospect of getting one, and I'm not doing anything coherent about it, nor am I filling my life up with anything else. But all that's not too bad. The bad thing is that I'm failing—I feel I'm failing—my son, Horace, who is seven years old. Seven and two thirds. There's a basic sense in which you want to protect your child, and I'm not doing it. I'd do anything for him. But I'm not doing anything. If you see what I mean.'

Henry paused. Where was he? Oh yes. Failing Horace.

'It's not that I think you'd fail at giving me what I want. I'm not even asking anything from you. What I want is a job. To get my life sorted out. To get my room cleared up with the right pieces of paper in the right piles, and the right people written off to. You can't give me any of that. My doctor can give me a simple pill that might put me in a position to get going again. That's all.'

'Perhaps you don't have enough illusions, Henry.'

What was her accent? It sounded half something odd, like Lebanese, and half something familiar, like Australian or South African.

'Maybe. I'm not sure that Lori would agree with you.'

'Perhaps you are too hard on yourself.'

'Oh, thank you, Natasha. That's very helpful of you. Now I feel a great deal better about my life. This really is a process that's going to do me a lot of good. I mean, sitting in a room sounding off is going to be terrific.'

Henry felt bad. He had been looking for somebody to shout at for months. Some people abused the officials down at the DSS, others wandered in the street muttering or yelling at strangers. If you were American, you took your gun out for a walk and shot some people from the company that fired you or commuters on the train that used to take you to work. White rage. He had spilt it out at this woman he'd never met before, and there it was on the carpet and it didn't quite look as though it belonged to him, like vomit once it has left your body. There are a few fragments of things you've eaten, and though you can vouch for the mixture in a general sort of way, most of it seems unfamiliar, and all of it smells disgusting. And he felt embarrassed. He was being drawn into conversation deliberately, lured into a process. He could watch it, but like an observer in a dream, he could not halt it.

In response to some further questions, Henry talked about this and that and then suddenly, to his great surprise, Natasha Kaposi spoke at length about what she felt about him.

'Henry, perhaps it would be good if I gave you my first feelings about what you have said. It is my view that when you describe your feelings about your son, it is really a way of talking about the failings, as you see them, of your relationship with your father. When you talk about your problems with your wife, it is the relationship between your parents when you were a child. Your wish to fill boots, to fit into a role that you think a man, or a father, or a husband, should play, comes from the people who created your ideas of those roles. That is, your parents, when you were a small boy. This is the area that I would like to explore with you in future sessions, and I should add that I think it necessary for you to come to see me three times a week.'

Henry twisted round on the couch to see if she was serious.

'How could I possibly do that?'

She was firm.

'Two sessions might just be possible, but inadequate in my opinion. One session would not give us the time to explore what needs to be explored if this treatment is to have value for you.'

'Is there any discount for bulk attendance?'

'No. I have limited time, which I could fill up twice over. And as you have already said, you have to be committed to this process, just as I have to be. You have to feel it is something that is worth paying for. Your money gives you a stake in taking the treatment seriously.'

Now there was a long silence while Henry performed some mental calculations.

'Let's be completely clear about this. If I were to do it, that would cost me a hundred and five pounds a week, and that's not including the travel from Hampstead, which is where I thought all therapists lived anyway, to Ladbroke Grove. Then there is the time. About three hours three times a week when I would be out of the house and would either have to arrange something for Horace or just leave Lori alone. In exchange for all of that, what can you offer me in return? I don't want a guarantee, I know all of that. What prospect can you offer me?'

Kaposi talked calmly. She had said all of this before. This was the patter of the saleswoman, confident that you were about to get the pen on to the dotted line for that extra policy or for the new extension that you hadn't thought you needed.

'What you will do is to talk. Your talk at the moment, your view of your life and your relationship, is like a collection of scattered impressions and feelings, bits of guilt and hope and failure. What we shall do is, as you said of your office at home, sort through them, put them into piles, throw away the ones we don't need, find some that had seemed to be lost, perhaps even obtain some new ones from outside, and then assemble them together into a unity. In the case of your room at home, it would be a functioning office, which serves its purpose unobtrusively. With respect to your talk, we shall take messy impressions, misconstructions, and make them into, shall we say, a story, a narrative in which the pieces follow one from the other, in which the motivation becomes clear, in which the characters make sense.'

'It sounds like the sort of old-fashioned story that I like to read.'

'I am not offering to make you happy, but you would gain some form of insight, which is in itself a form of control.'

Dear Ms Kaposi,

I have been thinking about our specimen session yesterday and I have decided not to proceed with the course of psychotherapy, which was anyway what I was intending in advance.

I know I was being argumentative, perhaps even confrontational in a way, but perhaps I was a bit cowardly, unable just to say that I don't want therapy, that it's not the right thing. The problem was, of course, that we couldn't talk about therapy because everything I said to you in your room was treated as part of the therapy. So if I had said this directly to you, you would have responded with something like, Why is it you feel that you do not wish to examine your life, is there something you are afraid of? And then I might have said, but I don't accept that the treatment is valid. To which you would probably have answered, let's talk about your reluctance to commit to this dialogue. And so on, *ad absurdum*. There is no language in which I can tell you that it's not for me. Even that statement you would no doubt consider some symptom of neurosis which is worthy of exploration. Irritating maybe (for me) but at least it won't cost me any money. I could add that I felt your instant analysis was both simplistic and simply wrong—what knowledge of my parents do you really have?—but I suppose there is no language in which I could convince you that any theory of yours about me is wrong. The very notion of such objective refutation must be unintelligible to you.

That's the problem, ignoring any other of the difficulties I may have. My situation is something like: a) I've lost my job; b) I'm worried about money, because we always struggle to get enough and I'm earning very little; c) this causes anxiety which d) probably causes the symptoms in my stomach. In my own opinion the best thing for me would be to get a job which would eliminate a, b, c and d one after the other, and I could probably get rid of d anyway for a short time with some pills or something. Your solution is not to offer to deal with a, b, d or even c, which you might at least expect to be in your department. Instead I will be paying £105 a week for the no doubt interesting prospect of talking about myself for an hour every couple of days to somebody who promises to pay attention. In the meantime, though, this will make b worse which will make c worse which will probably make d worse which is the whole reason I was diverted towards you in the first place.

To be less directly polite, do you really believe that it is responsible of you to suggest three-times weekly therapy for me when I've told you what my life is like? On the other hand, it may be that you know that the benefits of three hours a week with you are so great that they justify any sacrifice, even the risk it would pose to my marriage, the saving of which is surely a lot of what this is all about. If I ever get prosperous and have time on my hands, then I'll get back in touch and I'm sure there would be nothing I would like better than to consider myself at length.

In the meantime, I've just bought a tin of green figs in syrup and a small carton of cream, which irritatingly I've just discovered has got UHT written on the side. I've looked outside and although it's now the middle of October, the sun is shining brightly which makes the yellow leaves look golden. The sky is entirely clear, and I can see a jet, far away and high up in the blue, leaving no vapour behind it. We don't have a real terrace but we have a bit of roof with a railing which I can get out to from a window. I'm going to sit there for half an hour and eat the green figs with cream. The total cost will be about a pound and I think it will be better for me than an hour spent dredging up old grievances against my family.

I'm sorry I've written so much. But then it was inevitable because I've got something else I ought to be getting down to and it's quite urgent. As I told you I always find it easier to do the things I'm not supposed to be doing. I'll get down to it after I've eaten my figs.

I enclose a cheque for £35 (which I can ill afford). Now I suppose I can go to Dr Inglis and claim my drugs.

> Best wishes,
>
> Henry (Dean)

Dear Mr Dean,

Thank you for your cheque. I am sorry you have decided not to undertake weekly psychotherapy sessions.

> Yours sincerely,
>
> Natasha Kaposi

Part Two

1. In

HORACE DEAN WAS an ordinary seven-year-old boy, ordinary in every way, except for his name, which he detested and didn't deserve. He had no brothers or sisters but he had two friends. His best friend was called George, and his second best friend was called Ollie. George lived in a house which had a climbing-frame in the garden. You could climb to the top of it and see gardens for the whole length of the road. Ollie was missing the bottom part of his left leg and had an artificial foot and ankle attached to the point where his shin had given up all hope of proceeding further and had contracted slightly into a wedge shape before stopping altogether. George had his climbing-frame, but Ollie had his artificial foot. Casual observers would not have noticed it in action, disguised beneath Ollie's jeans and football socks and almost silent when in motion. Only initiates had seen it in its detached state, an awesome assembly of hollow plastic, with metal hinges and struts, fastened on to the stump of flesh by means of straps. Horace had once been allowed to hold Ollie's manufactured limb for a moment. He found it heavy and said so.

'It's just the same as a joined-on foot,' Ollie had said.

Horace had a mother, called Lori, who taught mathematics in a school, not Horace's school. He had a father, called Henry, who sat at home and worked in his study, though what he did in there was never much discussed. Horace was forbidden from entering when his father was working. He sometimes wondered what it could be that justified excluding him and when he was only a little bit younger he had imagined his father as a magician, uttering spells and concocting potions, surrounded by the tools of his necromantic trade: globes, coloured bottles, dusty and ancient leather-bound volumes, glass tubes holding bubbling liquid. Now he knew that there was nothing in there except papers, books and letters scattered across the floor. Occasionally, he would squeak the door open, and his father would be absorbed in something, lost from his son, reading a newspaper or riffling the pages of a paperback or sitting in silent thought.

His father would read him stories, in which his mother would take no interest. His mother would sit with him and play games or talk about figures and shapes that his father didn't understand. Henry explained to Horace that Lori didn't like stories that were just made up. Lori explained to Horace that numbers were a way of understanding the world, of making sense of it, of being at home in it.

'What about stories?' Horace had asked.

'Stories are like dreams,' she had replied. 'When you're asleep you tell stories to yourself. Then you wake up and have things changed?'

'No,' said Horace. 'Except that it's morning.'

'Stories are fun, but they're like dreams. When the story is over, nothing has changed.'

'Henry doesn't know about numbers, does he?'

'He knows a bit, but he doesn't really care about them. That's why he's frightened of getting on to aeroplanes. And Henry believes that you can find out about what's going to happen by looking up at points of light in the sky.'

Henry, who was sitting nearby, felt that this conversation was aimed as much at him as at Horace, or at least that he was liable to be struck by stray pieces of shrapnel.

'Don't be silly, Lori. They've done research and they did find some statistical correlation with astrological predictions. That's the sort of scientific proof you believe in, isn't it?'

'Henry, it's all right for you to make statements like that to me because I know they've got about as much intelligent content as the sound of the back door banging in the wind. Please don't say things like that in front of our son.'

Horace was occasionally called on to pass judgement on some of these disputes, or summoned as a witness, but he remained stubbornly above the fray.

'There are no triangles in nature,' his father had once said to him bafflingly as he sat with his mother considering a diagram.

'Nonsense,' his mother had replied. 'There are plenty of triangles in nature. We're a triangle. Look. There's one point. We'll call that Henry, though sometimes I wonder if there's any point to him at all. Here's another point, which we'll call Lori. Where do you want the third point to go? OK, we'll call that Horace. Now we'll draw a line from Horace to Lori and a line from Henry to Horace. And I suppose we'd better draw a line from Lori to Henry in order to make the triangle complete. There. That's a triangle.'

Horace rather enjoyed the arguments, which was something the three of them did as a family, or, rather, something Henry and Lori did while Horace looked on, sometimes admiring the passion and precision with which they fenced with each other. Horace also spent much of his time in what his father called 'the creative condition of boredom', a phrase which Horace didn't understand but which seemed to mean that Henry read a paper or watched television, with a disengaged air, as if he were looking through them at something else, or at nothing, while Lori rattled and banged things, sometimes vengefully, it sounded, on other floors.

Horace considered the house to be full of dull objects with tiresome primary functions which only adults would ever think interesting. Unknown to Henry and Lori, there was a ghost house occupying the same space as the tedious adult one, containing the same objects. The difference was that the ghost house was presided over by Horace, and every object in it had a different, deeper function than the linear predictability of its other state. These functions were not always obvious, even to Horace, and much of his home life was devoted to discovering precisely what they might be. Books were for piling up into castellated walls, behind which Horace crouched, hiding from the raking fire from a nearby machine-gun nest. Using the vacuum cleaner as a flame-thrower, he would raise himself above the line of the trench and roast the screaming enemies before they had time to fire back.

The coffee-table now functioned as a cable-car. Horace scrambled on the side of it as the exposed spy grabbed at his legs. Horace kicked hard, grinding the heel of his German army boot into the man's mouth, leaving it dripping with blood. The baddie's grip slackened. Take that. One further kick and he fell, his scream fading as he plummeted to the mountain below.

Cutlery was for dropping, piece by piece, on to the soft tile floor. The blades of the knives were inserted between tines of the forks, and they could then be assembled into a stun grenade which could be tossed at the wall, from where it could fall and shatter on the floor. At other times, objects would just inertly retain their adult meanings, and Horace would sullenly kick at them. A small rip of the wallpaper in the passageway, already flapping from some previous owner, had provoked surprising wrath from both his parents. His mother had shouted at him and then started to cry, ignoring Horace's protest that there was so much more of it, going down the stairs to the street and snaking round all the way up to the landing on the next floor.

One day, the day on which this whole story really

begins, a Saturday morning in October, a hot day, perhaps the last really hot day of the year, Horace was sitting upstairs in his bedroom contemplating his favourite inanimate friends, who were ranged on the rug before him, seated, their backs propped against the shelf behind them. In order of preference they were his bear, pummelled and flattened by seven years of violent affection, called Rob, which was short for Robinson; a rag doll, which despite the advice of various adults, Horace had resisted naming, and which he concealed from his friends, but which he adored; and thirdly, and finally, an ancient, threadbare dog whose eye-beads had long been lost or torn out and more recently replaced with two large buttons. They gave their new possessor an ambiguous expression which varied according to Horace's mood: docile, wise or ferocious. He was called Seamus, named after his grandparents' dog who, at the beginning of the year, had become ill and been taken away and killed.

As Horace addressed his friends with his characteristic form of monologue, he became aware of strange sounds from downstairs. At first they were unintelligible, but Horace soon recognized them as the voices of his parents, distorted by emotion.

'Stay where you are,' said Horace to Rob, the doll and Seamus, and left them in the room.

As he crept downstairs and drew closer to the area of apparent conflict, the voices became louder, but he was still unable to make out anything more than a few stray individual words. Reaching the ground floor, Horace stepped into the doorway and the noise ceased, as if a radio had been switched off. The faces of his parents turned towards him with startled expressions, like those of burglars who had been surprised. His mother was standing in the middle of the room, her face startlingly pale, which emphasized the fierce darkness of her eyes. Suddenly silent, she was breathing heavily, as if at the end of an intolerable physical exertion. His father was seated on the worn sofa under the window. His face, beneath his shaggy, blond hair, looked entirely different from hers: it seemed passive, receptive. His cheeks were florid. His hands were trembling. Lori visibly came to a decision, swept past her son, took her coat and left the house. Horace felt the slam of the door resonating under his feet.

Henry let his head sink down into his hands. After a few moments, he raised it and looked at his son with a partial smile. Horace thought he heard him whistling, without a tune, almost imperceptibly. He stood up and left the room, returning a few minutes with a drink already half gone. He lowered himself back into the sofa with a sigh.

'Come and sit beside me, Horace,' he said.

Horace joined his father, who smelt medicinal.

'Have you been having a good play upstairs? What did you play?'

Horace rarely answered direct questions and he just swung back and forth on the sofa, wondering how far forward he would have to lean before he fell off altogether. It didn't seem as if Henry would bother to pursue the matter. Another thought seemed to occur to him. He ruffled the hair at the back of Horace's neck in a manner that outraged him.

'You know, Horace, you're really a lucky little boy.'

'I'm not a little boy.'

'I know you're not little, really. But you're little compared to somebody big and grown up, like me. It seems hardly any time at all since you were just a tiny baby who couldn't talk. I used to be able to hold you on just one arm.'

This was not the way to win Horace round. He was quickly bored by talk about what he had been like as a baby, when he had walked, what his first word had been, the sweet mistakes he had made. Henry reverted to his previous subject—Horace's good fortune.

'What you don't know, Horace, what you can't know, is that nothing seriously bad has ever happened to us. Right now, just at the very moment we are speaking, there are people like you and me and Lori who have found themselves in the middle of wars. I know that you play games with your guns, but wars are nothing like your games. Houses are destroyed, and people have to leave their home towns or villages and go somewhere else and never come back, ever. They can be lucky to escape. Sometimes whole families can be blown up, or a little child like you can be left with no parents. There are children just like you who are in the middle of the war and have to find food and look after themselves completely on their own.'

Horace was icily, silently furious. His father clearly had no conception of what Horace's games were like. Henry took a deep gulp of his drink.

'Of course,' he continued, 'that's far away. It's not very likely that our house will get blown up. I don't want you to be worried about that. But there are people in this country, in this town, who don't have a house to live in. When it rains, you can look at the water splashing against the window. Cuddle up warm in your bed. Some people don't know at the beginning of the day where they'll be sleeping at the end. Some people have their houses taken away from them. You were born into this house, Horace, and you think it's just there. But some people can't pay for the places they're meant to live in, and the people they're meant to pay get crosser and crosser and in the end they come along and take all the things from inside, all the furniture and the toys, and throw them out on the street and lock the doors. We've always been all right in this house. And we're well. You've never been ill, have you, Horace?'

'I'm ill now.'

'Are you, my darling? What's wrong?'

'I've got an ache in my tummy and on my knee.'

'Did you fall over?'

'I think I did,' Horace replied carefully. 'I fell over in the playground yesterday, when I was being chased, but I don't know if that is where the hurt on my knee came from.'

'I'm sorry, Horace. But you know, the pain in your tummy and your knee will get better soon. Some people become ill and they never get better. They get iller and iller and they die, and nobody ever sees them again. Even some children get ill and have lots of pain and then they die. Not one of us, not me, not Lori, not you, has ever been really ill.'

'I had pox,' said Horace.

'Chickenpox. But that was good. You were lucky to get that when you were young and could hardly feel it. I got it when I was thirteen. I had spots like little itching volcanoes all over my body, even on my gums. Other places as well. There are other things apart from illnesses. You heard Lori and me shouting at each other just now, didn't you? Sometimes we have arguments about things. That's like when you want to have chocolate and we say you have to eat your supper and it's not possible to do both at once, so we sometimes have an argument about it and make you have your supper first. Sometimes Lori and I feel differently about things, and we think different things, and you can't think the two different things at the same time.'

'Why can't you?'

'Well, try it. Try and think of yourself at the seaside and in a museum at the same time.'

Horace paused, his face clenched in thought. He relaxed.

'Yes, I can,' he announced.

'No, you can't. It's impossible. Don't be so silly. You can't have two things in the same place at the same time.'

'You can. I thought of sand in a museum.'

'That's not at the seaside.'

'You can have a museum at the seaside.'

Horace looked as if he was about to cry.

'Look,' said Henry, 'the example isn't important. What I mean is that something can't be red and blue at the same time.'

'Yes, it can,' said Horace. 'It can be red in some bits

138

and blue in others. Or it could be reddy blue.'

'Well, I don't know anything about colours, I'm colour-blind, but that argument doesn't matter.'

'What's colour-blind?'

'It means you can't see colours.'

Horace became properly interested for the first time.

'Really? What colour's a postbox then?'

'Oh, God, Horace, all I was saying is that everybody has disagreements and you argue and perhaps you even shout at each other a bit. But some people can't manage that. They move on from shouting. They hit each other. They even decide that they can't live together. One of them leaves, and they have to split up everything, get rid of the house and move into two different houses. The point of all this, Horace, is that sometimes things seem difficult but really they're good. They're good compared with really bad things.'

'Where's Lori gone?'

Henry laughed.

'If you keep a fierce dog cooped up in a little space, it starts to go crazy. It howls and snaps and starts to knock furniture over and chew things up. You need to take it outside to a very large space where it can run around and howl at the moon. A long, long, long time ago, dogs were wild, and there's a little bit of them that still remembers it. And every now and then, they need to go outside and be a bit like a wild animal again. Lori's like that.'

'Is Lori going to howl?'

'I think she'll probably howl a bit.'

'Why can't she howl indoors?'

'She probably wants to howl where nobody can hear her. You need to be alone to howl properly. You can only do little howls in the flat.'

Henry gave a little cooing, bleating howl like a whipped mongrel.

'But proper howls are harder to do.'

Henry threw back his head and gave a hoarse whoop, incredibly loud, impressively sustained. For the first time, his son seemed shocked and impressed.

'Is that a real wolf howl?'

'Yes, it's the very particular howl that a wolf gives when he feels that things have gone completely wrong with his life and he doesn't know what to do about it.'

'How did you learn it?'

'A wolf taught it to me. Now, Horace, why don't you go off and play a game on your own for a bit while I finish my drink?'

Horace had listened to little of what his father had said and had been bored by most of what he had heard, except for the last bit and the bit about the postbox, so he agreed more quickly than he usually would have. He stood up and hopped out of the room, stepping from crack to crack of the floorboards. He leapt through the doorway into the hallway, skating across the smooth chessboard of tiles, his socks prickling. Once in the hall, he consulted his capacious repertory of games that could be played alone. His mental cursor slipped through the possible categories: wars, escapes, spaceships, adventures, quests, football without a ball, chess without a board or knowledge of the rules, castaway, shark, escape to another world. That sounded right. Highlight escape to another world and press the button.

He closed his eyes and stood upright, emitting a resonant hum. *Hmmmmm.* His lips itched.

'What are you doing, Horace?'

Horace ignored his father's question and cannoned between the wall and the staircase. The staircase. He opened the small door, cut in a triangular shape, the hypotenuse echoing the descent of the stairs. No other world in there. No forests or fields or strange, ancient halls. Just old umbrellas, a folded-up pushchair, rubber boots, indeterminate metal poles belonging to a tent, perhaps, or a paddling pool. In another mood, Horace might have pulled some of them out, or climbed inside the cupboard, enlisting these unused objects for an improvised construction. Now he was looking for an appropriate doorway.

Reaching the kitchen, he looked around. He slid open three cupboard doors, crammed with pots and the components of mysterious cooking equipment that Lori and Henry hardly ever used. Then he looked at the fridge. Most of the plastic letters on its façade had been pushed to one side as usual in a swirl of meaningless alphabet soup. In the centre of the door, just six letters remained, arranged in a row: inherE.

That was it, that was the sign, a message, perhaps even an order. Horace opened the fridge and looked inside. It was unpromisingly cluttered. The way would have to be cleared. From the two shelves, Horace removed a bowl of potatoes wrapped in polythene, a bowl of spaghetti now old and matted, a jar of pickled gherkins, a lump of hard, yellowed cheese, a bowl of sweet corn, six little plastic pots of fromage frais in assorted flavours joined together, a Soup of the Month, a carton of milk lying on its side, a plate containing some ancient fish balls (every time this dish was served, Henry used to ask what they did with the rest of the fish), another plate containing two cooked pork sausages, a bottle of white wine half full with the cork pushed back in. Right at the back, where there was something wrong with the cooling panel, stood a can of lager and a jar of sliced beetroot, both of them encased in ice and stuck. Horace tugged at them, and they came away with a splintering crack.

When he had placed all of the food on the kitchen floor, he slid out the two shelves. Now there was space. He stepped into the fridge and rapped his knuckles against the back. He waited a few seconds but nothing happened. Yet the instructions had been quite clear. He would have to demonstrate complete belief in what was about to happen. Horace recalled what his mother had told him about this old fridge. Never, never play with fridges. Children who lock themselves inside fridges like the one we have cannot get out and they can die. Well, he wasn't playing. Horace hooked his foot under the door and pulled it to. He had not gained enough leverage and it bounced back open. He put his fingers round the door pulling it closed with greater force. The fridge sealed itself with a resolute click, and Horace found himself in the dark.

2. By

HORACE WAS INTERESTED to discover that in the fridge there was not even a crack of light like the soft line along the bottom of his bedroom door. He closed his eyes and opened them again. There was no difference. With impressive speed, he felt the onset of cold. It must come from the back wall, where the ice had been. He stretched out his hand to touch it and found his hands—to his not very great surprise—punching into darkness. He reached around him in all directions and felt nothing but space. Though he was a little boy, not large even for his seven years, Horace had been compelled to crouch in order to fit inside the fridge. Now he stood up, and his head did not strike the roof. He gingerly extended his arms, expecting to scrape his fingers on a solid surface, but was unable to feel even the fridge door. After its brief chill, the air was now becoming warm once more.

He could still see nothing. The darkness was absolute. Horace had the impression that he could feel it between his fingers, that it absorbed all sound as well as light. Which way was up or down? He crouched and touched the ground by his feet. His fingertips felt rock with a thin layer of powder, or dust. So there was something, at any rate, but what was he to do now? He gave a muffled shout, but his voice seemed as incapable of penetrating the vacancy as his eyes, and there was no reply. He peered into the murk, and he was never sure afterwards whether it had been there all the time or gradually appeared, but he became aware of a very slightly lighter patch of blackness within the dark, a grey, cloudy area, and he began to make his way towards it, feeling in front of him for possible obstructions. He had no sense of moving up or down, or of distance, or of time, but without perceptible change the area he was making for became less oppressively black, then dark grey, light grey and then Horace walked into an island of lightness in a sea of nothingness; there was no lamp or window, no visible source of the light, or of heat, at all.

The light island measured just a few yards across and it illuminated nothing beyond its boundaries, but Horace was now able to see that at its far edge, perhaps twenty paces distant, was an imposing doorway, with no door. Horace walked across and peered through, but nothing was visible.

'Hello,' he shouted through it. 'Is anybody there?'

Horace's voice echoed as if it was in a large vault. He was startled by a croaking answer from close at hand.

'Wait a minute, don't rush me. Just make yourself comfortable. Sit down.'

Horace peered through the doorway for some evidence of the speaker.

'There's nowhere to sit,' said Horace.

But he looked around and there was somewhere to sit, two simple chairs next to a table. He obediently sat down in the chair which faced the doorway. He was curious and scared about what might appear, but it would have been more frightening for whatever it was to come from behind. To nudge him on the shoulder, or worse. He heard the sound, not of footsteps exactly, but more like the soft padding of a large animal, and a man stepped out of the darkness through the doorway and into the light. He was a tall man with a bald head, a long, sharply pointed nose and a dark beard, long strands of which descended from his chin. All that was visible of his clothes was the long fur coat wrapped about his body and the carpet slippers on his feet. Catching sight of Horace, he paused and scrutinized him, tipping his head backwards as if to align his sight along the incline of his nose.

'Who are you?' he demanded, firmly, though not unkindly.

'What do you mean, who am I?'

'Well, what are you called?'

'Horace.'

'Hmm.' The man seemed dissatisfied. 'That's a funny sort of name. It's the sort of name given to boys long ago who played with boxes of matches or who got eaten by a lion at the zoo.'

'I knew that already,' said Horace. 'You didn't have to tell me that.'

'Don't worry. I rather like it, probably more than you do. It is a survivor from a better time. An age of servants in terraced houses, cooks, horse-drawn carriages, governesses, absent parents, magic carpets and wishes. But then, I am an old man.'

He waited for a response, but Horace's attention had wandered. The man had become boring and then entirely incomprehensible, and Horace had other things to think about.

'That means that, like many people, I think that things used to be better.'

'Who are you?'

'I am the keeper of the gate.'

'No, I meant what is your name?'

'I don't need a name. There's nobody here to call me anything. Just you, and I don't expect you to confuse me with anybody else.'

There was a long silence, and the gatekeeper seemed as unconcerned by this as the door-frame. He was not embarrassed, he was not curious, he was not cross, he was not expectant.

'We will strike a bargain, Horace,' he finally said. 'You will ask me a question, and I will ask you a question. We will each, of course, undertake to respond to the questions.'

Horace looked puzzled.

'I mean, we each promise to answer the question.'

'What sort of question?'

'That, for example, is a sort of question. But I will allow you another chance. Try to think of a question that will be more helpful.'

'Can I ask for something?'

'If you like. And I shall allow yet another question to do so, if that's what you want.'

Horace thought of what he might possibly want, and recalled his entrance into this black world through the fridge.

'I'd like breakfast.'

The gatekeeper laughed, evidently surprised.

'What a surprisingly sensible request. What do you have for breakfast?'

'I'd like a bowl of Coco Pops with milk. Bacon and eggs and tomatoes and mushrooms. And baked beans. And tomato ketchup. Croissants and toast with marmalade and jam and honey. Orange juice made out of real oranges. Please.'

The gatekeeper gave a dry grimace.

'How do you like your eggs cooked, Horace?'

'Fried.'

'Sunny side up?'

'Sunny side down.'

The gatekeeper gave a grunt and shuffled back into the darkness. He returned almost immediately with a tray bearing the cereal and an earthenware jug of creamy milk, warm, winking with bubbles. He sat and watched Horace emptying the bowl then, when it was almost empty, left and returned with the cooked breakfast.

'Don't touch the plate. It's hot.'

He left again and returned with the toast, the croissants and three small white dishes in which were soft yellow butter, strawberry jam and orange marmalade with thick lumps of peel, just the way Horace didn't like it. He painstakingly removed the strands before spreading the marmalade on the toast. Horace pointed out that there was no tomato ketchup, and the gatekeeper sighed and disappeared. On his return, Horace was disappointed to see that the ketchup was manufactured by a company he had never heard of, the sort of own-brand version that his parents had the irritating habit of buying. The gatekeeper sat on the chair opposite. He ate nothing and drank nothing. Horace was surprisingly hungry. He had wondered at first whether his breakfast would taste of anything, whether it would be real, but after he had poured the milk on his cereal, tipped the jam on a croissant, cut up the bacon and dipped it into the stabbed fried egg, it tasted recognizably enough like the sort of food that he really did have for breakfast, though he had never had all of it at once before. Perhaps it tasted a little stale, as if it had been kept too long, or as if Horace had been long expected and had arrived late. He spoke with his mouth full, but the gatekeeper did not seem to be the sort of adult who bothered about things like that.

'Do you have a cow and a kitchen and things like that out there?'

The gatekeeper smiled and shook his head.

'Then what's through that doorway?'

'It seems to me, Horace, that you are doing all the asking, and I am doing all the answering. That is a difficult question to answer in ways that you would understand. There is wearisomeness, painfulness, hunger, perils, nakedness, sword, lions, dragons, darkness. That sort of thing.

Are you enjoying your breakfast, your second breakfast of the day, no doubt?'

'It's great, thanks. What's "sword"?'

'I think it's time for me to ask my question, though it's really more like a game. What I would like, Horace, is for you to tell me everything that you can think of that frightens you. You don't have to tell me what frightens you most. Just tell me the sort of things that come into your head when you think of fear. That is, when you think of being frightened.'

'I know what fear means,' said Horace a little crossly, but he was pleased as well because he liked lists, even if he generally disliked being cross-examined. But this was different. A quiz. He prided himself on being good at things like that.

'Vampires, they're frightening.'

'Are they really?' the gatekeeper mused dubiously. 'I wonder whether you are really frightened of them, or whether they are the sort of thing that you think *ought* to be frightening. The sort of thing that somebody like me might expect you to say. Think harder.'

'Vampires *are* frightening. They bite your neck and suck out your blood. Poisonous snakes. They leap at you faster than you can run away and there is poison in their teeth. And lions and tigers. Going into the woods and fighting a great bear. Being underwater and drowning. Having to jump off a skyscraper. Falling off a cable-car. The dark, when you don't know what's there, or what might be coming. A real war, not a play one. A car crash. Going across the road when cars are driving along it.

Monsters coming in the dark. Going across a train track at night. One of those places where there are lots of different tracks next to each other. And you can see the light of a train coming but you can't tell which track it's on. And whichever way you go, you can't get away from it. Running away from a crocodile, or trying to swim away from a crocodile and knowing that you can't go fast enough and wondering if you'll get to the side in time. Touching fireworks when they might be about to go off. Loud bangs when you're not expecting them. Jumping out of a window. Walking on a roof, one of those roofs with a steep slope, slipping down and down, and over the edge and trying to hold on to the edge with your hands and then just fingers and knowing that you can't hold on. Being lost. Someone forcing you to have a fight with them. A seed pushed up your nose.'

'What do you mean, "a seed pushed up your nose"? Do you mean that it starts to grow there, or is it just that it feels uncomfortable?'

Horace shrugged and gesticulated, but he had just returned to his croissant and he was unable to speak. It was in any case not the sort of question that he would have bothered to answer. With a gulp and a gasp he swallowed his last mouthful. The lower half of his face was now smeared with grease and flakes of pastry.

'I've finished.'

'Good,' said the gatekeeper. 'Let me wipe your face before we do anything else.'

He raised his hand and rotated a damp cloth round Horace's grimacing face, over his forehead, into the crevices of his closed eyes and around his mouth, under the chin to the neck and then into the ears. So that sort of thing happened here as well. The cloth was flipped over and used to dry him. Horace surveyed the remnants of his breakfast.

'What do I do now?' he asked.

'What do you want to do?'

'I don't know.'

The gatekeeper ran his fingers down through his beard.

'Perhaps if you knew why you were here, you might know what you wanted.'

Horace neatly piled the plates one on top of the other so that the clean undersides became stained by the soiled plate beneath. 'May I get down?'

'You don't need to ask stupid questions like that, not here,' said the gatekeeper, sounding sly and cruel for the first time. 'I don't care whether you get down or not.'

Horace felt hot in his cheeks, a prickling around his sinuses and in the corners of his eyes. He wondered whether to feel scared or not.

'I said, may I get down, because I've got to get home.'

'Where's home?'

'Don't be stupid, it's where I've come from. Back there.'

The gatekeeper looked impassive.

'Back where?'

Horace pointed away from the doorway, back into the darkness. He stared as if he were trying to see to the bottom of a deep, cloudy lake. Perhaps it was because his eyes were dazzled by the sourceless light, but he could see nothing.

'I want to go home.'

The gatekeeper lifted the pile of plates and began to walk towards the doorway, speaking as he did so.

'That didn't take long. You have already decided what it is that you want.'

He disappeared through the doorway. There was no sound of clattering cutlery and china, but a few seconds later he returned without the breakfast things. With his cloth he wiped away the crumbs and grease, the wet circles of juice, from the table.

'All we need to do now,' he said, 'is decide how you can achieve your wish. How you can get home.'

'That's easy,' said Horace, trying not to let his voice shake. 'All you need to do is show me the way out, back over there. Then I can find my way to the flat.'

'Have you ever seen a lobster-pot?' asked the gatekeeper. 'Perhaps you have never seen a lobster. It is an apparently fearsome crustacean, but surprisingly easy to trap. From the outside of the pot, the entrance is vast, but it shrinks as the lobster crawls down. The lobster squeezes through the aperture in order to reach some illusory reward and once inside it is impossible for him to escape the way he entered. You, Horace, have entered this island of light much like a lobster into a pot. There is one way in, but you could wander in the darkness for ever looking for the same way out again, and perhaps finding your way back would do you no good even if you managed it. Where were you at the moment you entered this darkness?'

'Inside a fridge. I'd pulled the door shut behind me.'

The gatekeeper shook his head and tutted in disapproval.

152

'Perhaps you are better off here than there. In any case, the only escape is in the opposite direction, through the doorway.'

Horace ran forward and stood by one of the pillars and stared through hopelessly.

'But that looks like the wrong way. Where does it go to?'

The gatekeeper shrugged, but before responding he walked around the table straightening the two chairs so that they stood straight, facing each other.

'You can wander back into the darkness, or you can stay here in the light seated at my table, or you can go through the doorway.'

'But what do I get to through the doorway? How do I know where to go? I can't do that, I don't know what to do.'

'I can tell you nothing, or almost nothing. I have never been anywhere but here, in or around or near the gate. Perhaps you would like to stay here. It will never change, but there will always be food on the table when you want it, and we do have some limited facilities. Will your home and family be any better than that?'

'Don't be silly, I can't stay here. I'm little, I have to go home. Can't you get me there?'

'I don't know. I'm just a door-keeper. I don't know the way to your home, but there is only one way out, so that is the way that you will have to take. Look through the doorway.'

'I have looked. I couldn't see anything.'

'You have not looked properly. Come, Horace. Stand

by me and try harder.'

Horace stepped forward and took the gatekeeper's hand. He stared so intently that his eyes ached.

'Do you see a little wicket-gate, far, far away?'

'What's that?'

'A small gate in a wall.'

'No, I don't,' said Horace.

'Oh, dear, I thought you'd be able to see a gate. Well, do you see a shining light, then?'

'I don't know,' said Horace, 'I think I can see a glow.'

And indeed, in the far distance, or maybe just small and faint in the darkness, there was a light, not like a spotlight illuminating the doorway, not like the moon, dimly radiant, but like a star, visible but not enough to illuminate anything.

'Keep that light in your eye,' said the gatekeeper. 'And go directly towards it. Then you will see the gate.'

'What do you mean, keep it in my eye? I don't know the way, I don't know what to do. Won't you come along with me?'

'My place is by this door. I have always been here and I must not leave it.'

Horace gave up. He sat on the ground and cried so that his whole body shivered with it. He raised his hands to his eyes and could feel the tears hot on his fingertips. He was aware of nothing for a time but as he collected himself, he saw that the gatekeeper had not reacted in any way. Horace wiped his tears away and spoke more fiercely.

'I can't go on my own. I'll get lost or go wrong. Can't somebody come along with me?'

'Perhaps. Think, Horace, who are your friends? Don't say anything, just think about those whom you trust. Listen.'

Horace was confused but he tilted his head, hearing sounds approaching in the darkness. He swivelled on his heels trying to establish where they were coming from. Three familiar figures emerged from the darkness on the far side of the light island from the doorway.

'Hello, Horace,' said one of them in a husky voice that Horace had never heard before.

Horace wasn't able to speak.

'Come on, you little idiot, say something.'

'Hello, Robinson,' said Horace.

'Aren't you going to introduce us?' said the gatekeeper.

'How can I introduce you?' said Horace. 'I don't know your name.'

'I don't have a name. I am what I do. You may introduce me as the gatekeeper.'

'All right.'

Horace pointed at the first of the new arrivals.

'This is my bear. He's called Robinson. And that's my toy dog, who is called Seamus.'

He paused, at a loss for a moment.

'That's a doll that I have. It doesn't have a name. I suppose that they're all here to help me.'

'Oh yes?' said Robinson. 'And who's the old guy?'

'He doesn't have a name. He's the gatekeeper.'

The three toys, if that was what they still were, did not look as they had when Horace had last seen them, crammed into the corner of his bed, and he wondered whether he had taken proper care of them. He had just been used to having them around. They were now bigger, of course. They wouldn't have been much help at their original size. Robinson and the doll were at least a foot taller than Horace, and even Seamus was the size of a large puppy. They were different in other ways as well, though it was hard to decide exactly how. These seemed like the real things of which, as Horace's toys, they had just been the imitation. Robinson had a touch of wildness about him, a different sheen to his fur; he had teeth and they looked sharp. His legs and arms were jointed and flexible. The doll was looking at Horace with suspicion. Seamus had spent much of his previous life with his legs twisted round the wrong way, but now every muscle was taut, and there was a visible quiver running from his damp nose down to the fur on his stubby tail. Robinson seemed to be the leader, so Horace addressed him.

'So, are you going to take me back home?'

'Fuck off.'

There was a terrible silence.

'Did I say that?' said Robinson, then laughed wheezily. 'What I meant was, of course we will. Here we've got a couple of animals and a strange nameless woman in charge of a little child. What else would we do? We wouldn't eat him, would we, Seamus?'

'We might eat him,' said Seamus. 'Nice fresh young meat. We like it raw and bloody. A bit stringy though— catches in the teeth.'

'You can't eat me,' said Horace. 'You're my toys. You belong to me.'

'Don't try that one on us, little boy. Look at Seamus. Not exactly a Crufts candidate. What if we just promise to look after you the way you looked after us? We won't lose you but we may knock you about a bit, crush you, pull your eyes out. And we'll replace them with nice new buttons if you like.'

'You've got to help me. That's what you were brought here for. You were the people I trusted.'

'That's pretty pathetic, isn't it?' said the doll, speaking in a murmur, as if the experience were new to her. 'Don't you have any real friends who could come and help you out? I suppose not. There's the one-legged one. He wouldn't be much good in a crisis. I'm not sure there's any of them you could really trust anyway. Look at that George. He's been playing a bit too much with Chris and Lester recently, I'd say. What do you think, Horace? Do you think they'd come through for you in a crisis, all those friends of yours?'

Horace stood numbly silent. What could he say?

'I didn't mean to hurt any of you.'

'Oh, shut up,' said Robinson. 'We're all thinking.'

He turned to the gatekeeper.

'I suppose we go through this doorway. What then?'

The gatekeeper shrugged.

'There is a road. Follow it and don't leave it.'

'He said we should go towards a light,' said Horace. 'Then what?'

'I don't know,' said the gatekeeper.

'That's not much use, is it?' said Robinson. 'Has anybody else got a suggestion?'

Seamus and the doll stayed silent.

'We could give her a name,' suggested Horace.

Robinson gave a grunt.

'All right, for want of anything useful to do.'

'What name?' she asked doubtfully.

'How about Lori?' said Horace.

'That's your mother's name,' said Robinson. 'We don't want to cause unnecessary confusion. Think of something else.'

Horace thought once more. Nobody else looked as if they were trying at all.

'What about Mary?'

'That's a bit boring,' said the doll. 'Do I look like a Mary?'

She stood and spread her dress on either side of her legs and tipped her head as she pondered it.

'I don't think she looks like a Mary,' said Robinson. 'She looks like a shabby toy that's been left out in the rain. What do you think, Horace?'

'No, she doesn't. What about Marie? That's a nice name.'

'Oh yes,' said Robinson. 'That's got a certain continental sophistication. That's about her level. I think she can settle for that.'

The doll thought and gave a smile.

'All right. Marie,' said Marie. 'That will do.'

'What about him, while we're at it?' said Robinson, gesturing at the gatekeeper. 'We could give him a name as well. Useless Prat would be about right.'

Horace giggled.

'I'm sorry, Horace, was I saying something funny?'

'Yes.'

'Well, I wasn't, so shut your mouth. Has anybody else any stupid comments to make? No? Good.'

Robinson paced around the confines of the light space as if it were a cage.

'Can anybody suggest anything apart from going through that door? Silence. Christ, what a collection of airheads. A doll and a dog. All right, Grandad, we're off.'

He turned to Horace who was looking at him expectantly.

'All right, you can tag along. Just don't cause any trouble.'

'Hold on a minute,' said the gatekeeper. 'Before you go, I think you all ought to shake hands. I'm not sure that you've all been very nice to Horace. He called you here as the three people in the world that he most trusts.'

'That's his problem,' said Robinson. 'I'm not interested in any of that "all for one" crap. I don't see what's in any of this for the bear. If Horace thinks that he can get home by hitching a ride with us, then he can get on with it, but it doesn't mean we're going to be taking showers together. So now, where do we go?'

'Where else but through the door? Keep to the road.'

Robinson gave a sarcastic grunt.

'I think I've managed to memorize all of that, so I suppose we had better set off. Are we all ready? Marie, are you looking beautiful enough to go out? Seamus, is your coat brushed? Claws clipped? Buttons polished? And Horace. Gone to the lavatory? Washed your hands? Warm sweater on? Laces tied? Hair brushed? Have you scrubbed behind your ears and under your fingernails? I've never understood the symbolic importance accorded to the small, inaccessible and scarcely visible area behind the flap of the ear, but we never know whom we might run into.'

'I didn't know there was a toilet here.'

The gatekeeper gave an embarrassed shrug.

'Nobody's ever asked before.'

'Oh, for fuck's sake, go in the dark somewhere,' said Robinson. 'As long as it's out of smelling distance. I don't suppose we'll be coming back. Give him some paper or something, Grandad.'

Marie pulled a couple of sheets of kitchen roll from the pocket of her dress and handed them to Horace, who then stepped into the dark. As he squatted, out of the sight of the others, apparently, he saw the gatekeeper leave and then heard his three companions talking among themselves, though he was unable to understand what they were saying. The gatekeeper returned carrying a tin bowl of steaming water, a navy-blue towel draped across one arm. He laid the bowl down on the table and beside it the towel and a cake of yellow soap. Horace carefully tore each sheet of kitchen roll in two, wiped himself, pulled up his trousers and returned into the light.

'If you will just wash your hands,' said Robinson, 'we can be on our way. Any remaining questions that occur to you had best be posed without delay.'

Picking up the soap, Horace plunged his hands into the bubbling, creamy, warm water and on an impulse lifted two handfuls up to splash and rub his face with it.

He felt for the towel and rubbed his closed lids.

'Can we come back here if we lose our way?' Horace asked.

'You can no more come back through the door than you can return to today if you find yourself disliking tomorrow.'

'But tomorrow will be today tomorrow,' said Marie. 'And today will be yesterday. You can never return to yesterday because yesterday is a relative term. You might as well have asserted that we can never go from here to there because once we arrive there it will be our here and what was our here has become our there. So your example is a faulty one.'

'Faulty or otherwise, you will not be able to return through this door once you have passed through. But then, what is there to return for?'

'Not for information, at any rate, or the pleasure of your company,' said Robinson. 'Have you any more verbal quibbles, Marie, that you wish to make before we leave?'

Marie grimaced at Robinson but said nothing.

'What about food for the journey?' asked Horace.

'We don't need food,' said Robinson.

Horace and his three toys approached the doorway.

'Straight through and towards the light,' said the gatekeeper. 'And don't leave the path, or you may never find your way back. It's even worse than here. Here it's just darkness.'

Horace, poised at the very edge of the doorway, looked at Robinson.

'How can I trust you?'

'What's there to trust? We're just toys. What could we do to you, except perhaps prevent you from returning home and carrying on torturing us? If you don't want to come, then stay here with baldy. We don't care. Or if you want, you can fuck off along the path on your own.

'There's nothing else I can do,' said Horace. 'I've got to come with you.'

'Then come.'

'Oh, all right,' said Horace.

He stepped through the doorway.

3. Through

'WHAT CAN YOU see, Horace?'

'You can see as well as I can.'

'Just tell us and stop pratting about.'

'Buildings. We're in a city, I think.'

'A big city?'

'It looks very big. Like London. It's the sort of place I live in.'

'Then I'm glad I've spent my life in a little boy's bedroom. Is it day or night?'

'I can't tell. It's grey and dark. I can't see the sun.'

'What else can't you see?'

'What do you mean?'

'Just answer.'

'I can't see lots of things. I can't see a rhinoceros. I can't see a firework. I can't see a football match.'

Robinson grabbed him firmly by his hair, twisting the strands in his fingers so that Horace's head was fixed in front of Robinson's own.

'That, Horace, is for being boring and irritating. Since you're being so stupid, I'll try to make it easier for you. Can you see any people?'

'No.'

'Can you see any signs of life, lights in windows, smoke coming out of chimneys?'

'No.'

'None of which matters, of course. The only question that matters is, can you see our path?'

'I can't move. Let me go. Yes. I think we're on it. It goes along by the river.'

'Does the river look to you as if it is in motion, Horace? Are there eddies and currents?'

Still gripping Horace's hair, Robinson held him out over the water. Grey and purple flowers of oil stained the surface.

'It's not moving at all.'

'This was built by somebody, Horace. A river that is built by somebody is called a canal.'

'I knew that.'

'You should have said so then.'

They seemed to have emerged from a tunnel on to the tow-path. Marie had wandered ahead and she turned back:

'Not exactly worth a detour. Do you think this is a happy city, Horace?'

Robinson released his hold. Horace looked around. The surface of the brickwork that lined the side of the path was furry black. Further up, far beyond reach, were stained, opaque windows. Nothing looked as if it worked or opened or functioned in any way. If they were warehouses, they were empty. If they were factories, they were abandoned. Horace felt he would have given anything for the glow of a furnace, for one chimney vomiting smoke. He slowly shook his head.

'Where are the people?' he asked.

'What people?' said Robinson. 'Perhaps there were never any people. Perhaps it was built like this, just for us. Our special city to wander through.'

'It doesn't look much cared for. I think we'll be able to resist the temptation to wander off,' said Marie. 'Fancy a swim, Horace?'

'I can't swim.'

She knelt down and dipped her hand in the water.

'What's it like?' asked Robinson. 'Nice and warm.'

Marie shook her head.

'Cold. Slimy. Not for paddling in unless desperate. I suggest that we start walking, unless anybody has an alternative plan.'

'We could toss Horace into the water and see if it's poisonous,' said Robinson, 'but then we'd only have to fish him out or listen to his screams. Not much of a place, but good for disposing of a body. Shove it in a hole somewhere, slip it into the water weighed down with a few stones. Let's go, then. If we're going.'

The path would have been wide enough for Robinson, Horace and Marie to walk side by side, but they rarely did. Robinson slouched with his hands in his pockets, often muttering to himself, and Horace didn't dare to attempt conversation. Seamus snuffled in front or skulked behind. Marie surprised Horace by taking his hand in hers, but this may just have been in order to hurry him along because he repeatedly stopped to contemplate a loose brick on the path, or rattle the padlock on a door, or peer through railings. They walked in silence past mile after mile of defunct, smoky, deserted buildings. There was no sound, not even the smallest lap of the water in its cracked stony course, and no wind.

'Who built all this?' asked Horace finally. 'And where have they gone? It's such a terrible place.'

'Nobody *builds* cities,' said Marie. 'They just get there, like valleys and mountains.'

'You're probably to blame for this one,' said Robinson, looking at Horace.

'No, I'm not,' said Horace.

'Well, it's not my idea of a city,' said Robinson. 'I could have come up with somewhere more pleasant than this.'

Anything that was said seemed to disappear into the cracks in the crumbling buildings and the spaces between them. It didn't seem a place for talking in, and the walkers lapsed into a silence which only Horace made an occasional effort to break.

'Are we getting anywhere?' he asked.

There was no reply.

'I said, are we getting anywhere?'

'I'm sorry,' said Robinson, 'I thought somebody said something incredibly stupid and pointless that wasn't worth bothering with.'

But they *were* getting somewhere. The canal's path now ran through a deep embankment, and bulging brick walls towered above them on either side. If the landscape had been crumbling before, it was now collapsing. The walls were scarred with deep cracks, and the path was covered with fallen bricks and fragments of concrete that had peeled off from the wall above and tumbled down. They turned a corner, and the canal came to a disastrous end in a huge mess of rubble, as if the two walls had given up entirely and fallen together in a heap. Seamus ran forward and sniffed at the colossal obstruction. The other three placed their palms on the fragments of brickwork and concrete as if feeling for a way through.

'Something's gone wrong with the plan,' said Marie. 'There must have been an earthquake and the path has been blocked.'

'It can't have gone wrong,' said Robinson. 'There must be a way through.'

'I don't know what you mean by must,' said Marie. 'Nothing else in this pit seems to be functioning, so I don't understand your trust in the walking facilities.'

She sat on a stone and pushed a finger into one of her soft shoes, rubbing the instep.

'We can stay here. We can climb over, or go round, or go back.'

'We can't climb over,' said Robinson, stepping back and looking up at the shattered slope which rose sharply and disappeared into the darkness. 'I couldn't get up that on my own, let alone with a kid and a dog. I suppose we could head back into this lovely town and try to come round in a big circle, though fuck knows where that would take us. I reckon we should just go back.'

Horace, who was sitting in sullen isolation at a distance,

raised his head when he heard that.

'We can't go back. We have to go on.'

Robinson turned his head sharply towards Horace, then spoke as if he hadn't heard.

'We'll go back the way we came and then perhaps the path will take us out of the city the other way.'

Horace stepped forward. He was scared and on the verge of tears.

'We've got to go on.'

Robinson turned and jabbed Horace in the chest so sharply that he stumbled backwards.

'Why should we?'

Horace's breath was coming in gulps, and he could barely speak.

'You were brought here to help. We've got to find a way through.'

Robinson looked pensive. Horace stepped down the path, out of range of his fists. Robinson visibly made up his mind.

'OK,' he said with cruel politeness. 'You're in charge, Horace. Show us the door, and we'll go through it.'

'Actually,' said Marie, 'there *is* a sort of door.'

'What do you mean?'

'Look.'

The canal came suddenly to an end, dammed by rubble, but to one side, a steady trickle of water leaked out and ran along a gully into an aperture no more than a couple of feet across in the great brick and concrete mass obstructing their progress.

4. Inside

'WE COULD TEST it,' said Robinson. 'We could shove Horace into the hole like a canary. If he comes back alive, then it's safe for the rest of us. What do you think, Seamus?'

Seamus gave a low growl.

'Horace is of more use to us alive,' said Marie. 'What will become of us if he drowns?'

'What will fucking well become of us whatever happens?' asked Robinson.

She shrugged. The four of them slid down the gravelly slope into the shallow gully where the water was flowing through a bed of pebbles. The wet ones gleamed with bright colours. Horace was tempted to pick one up and pocket it but he knew that it would be dry and grey when he got it home. The water ran for barely twenty yards, then disappeared between cracked slabs of concrete. They all gathered round this small black mouth, Seamus sniffing and splashing in the water.

'Here's your door,' said Robinson. 'After you.'

Horace felt hot, sick.

'I don't want to go in there.'

Robinson laughed.

'Are you scared, little boy? That nice old man said we have to follow the path.'

'It doesn't look like a path to me.'

Robinson knelt in the shallow water by the hole and inserted his head. The others heard a muffled yell. He looked back up at them.

'I can't see anything, but I suppose that's the way we'll have to go.'

He saw the look of dismay on Horace and Marie's faces and laughed.

'All right, it's dark and narrow and we'll probably be underwater for most of it. We may drown. But it's better than sitting listening to Horace's conversation.'

'I can't go in there,' said Horace. 'I just can't.'

'All right,' said Robinson. 'You stay here on your own.'

Horace took a deep breath.

'All right. I'll come.'

'Then let's do it quickly,' said Marie. 'One after the other. I'll go first. And do hurry.'

Marie crossed her arms, grasped the bottom seam of her dress and lifted it over her head. She was now wearing just tights and knickers visible inside them. Horace stared at her breasts, which had seemed flat as the dress was being removed, but became softer and rounder as she dropped her arms. The nipples stood out darkly against the blue paleness of her skin. She looked at Horace and their eyes met.

'My dress would probably snag on something and drown us all, don't you think, Horace?'

'Maybe.'

Marie smiled and looked down at her body.

'Oh, fuck it.'

She stepped out of her tights and knickers, revealing the shock of dark hair between her legs.

'What do you think? Sexy, eh?'

Horace didn't answer. She tied her clothes into a bundle and walked forward to the aperture. As she looked inside, she laid the bundle down, took a pin from her hair, wound up the longer curly dark strands at the back of her head and fastened it once more.

'I don't suppose there's much of a trick to this.'

She took her bundle and sat in the stream with her back to the hole. She took a few deep breaths, lay back and began to push herself into the tunnel, her feet wide apart to gain purchase on the slimy stones. She wriggled into the tunnel and was gone. Horace watched her disappear with a choking sensation in his chest, of mingled fear and excitement.

Seamus splashed into the stream and followed her. Horace heard Robinson cursing under his breath, as if shouting at himself made him feel better. Robinson yelled as he lowered his back into the stream and forced himself through the gap. Then it was Horace's turn, Horace who couldn't swim and who had refused even to go to a swimming-pool since the time he had slipped while jumping into the water and split open his forehead on the edge. He had let himself sink down into the water, helpless, until he was pulled out. Then he had felt the blood pulsing out of his head and watched the pale pink diluted liquid dropping on to the grainy, tiled floor.

Horace lay back in the stream, and the iciness of the water stung his back. Using his elbows and his feet, he pushed himself backwards, feeling the pebbles against his soaked shirt. The course of the stream led slightly downwards, so after just a few yards Horace saw the hole of dim light narrow and disappear between his feet.

'Hello, Rob,' he called. 'Are you there?' His voice seemed muffled in the darkness.

'No, I thought I'd take a detour to get a drink. Where do you fucking think I am? And that's Robinson to you. And don't do anything stupid like grabbing hold of my feet.'

Horace extended his right hand ahead and felt only air. He scrambled forward until he felt the texture of Robinson's rubber soles on his fingertips. The roof was getting lower as they moved further in, and after a few minutes, Horace's face was scraping on the crumbly pitted roof of the tunnel, which was invisible in the darkness. The stream was a trickle, a few inches deep, and the passage not much more than a foot high and barely wider than the span of his outstretched elbows. Horace thought of the tons of rock stretching on all sides of him, precariously balanced, one edge on another, looking for ways to fall and settle. He felt an urge to scream and struggle out towards any possible open space. What would happen if there was a sudden increase in the volume of water? A sudden fall of rain would drown them.

The water became deeper as the space shrank around him with every movement forward. The sour, damp dust stung his nostrils. Even when he pressed his face against the roof, Horace could feel the steely, cold water level with his ears. He collided with Robinson, who was moving back towards him.

'The water touches the ceiling ahead,' said Robinson, his voice echoing tinnily. 'But Marie and Seamus have gone on anyway. No fucking around.' He was panting now. Was he scared? 'Take a deep breath and rotate your body, which will take you right under the water. You probably won't die, unless you panic. Pity you can't swim. See you on the other side, maybe. Or feel you, anyway.'

As Horace eased himself forward, he heard a few deep breaths and felt Robinson's shoes turn, then move quickly forwards and away. Silence. He was on his own. He heard dripping. The water was close to the roof, the gap between them scarcely greater than the length of his nose. One two three four five. They must all be on the other side now, and he was left here, separated from them by a tunnel full of water. Six seven eight nine ten. He tried to take deep breaths. What would happen if he died here? A last breath of air, and he rotated, pushing himself under the water and forwards.

The problem was his buoyancy. Horace had to pull himself forward, holding on to the rock at the bottom or on the sides, scraping his elbows. A tube of water behind and in front of him. Suddenly, his progress was obstructed. He reached forward with his hands and felt Robinson's feet. He was stuck. Horace pushed at them but there was no movement away from him. Was Robinson dead? Should he wait for him to be rescued? What number was he at? Could he get back? Horace could feel that Robinson's shoes were flexed against the walls as he tried to push himself forwards, but the tunnel was so narrow by now that he could hardly bend his knees.

Horace couldn't bear it any longer. He pushed his way back down the tunnel the way he had come, more slowly this time, counting as he went. Twenty-five thousand twenty-six thousand twenty-seven thousand. Going more slowly. Have to allow more time. He forced himself to wait till thirty-five thousand, then rotated and pushed his face up at the roof. No air. A mouthful of metallic water. His chest was burning. Lights flared yellow behind his closed eyelids. He pushed himself back down, helped by the slight slope, and then heard a lapping as the water separated itself from the tunnel roof. A few more pushes, and his whole face was above the water.

Horace felt his chest splutteringly empty itself into the air through his mouth. He was gasping, shivering and sobbing all at once. He was in freezing water, in complete darkness, with an inch of air between the water and the stone, and a dead body ahead of him. He wanted to vomit. He wanted to scratch against the wall to get out of this trap, but the very restriction of his air supply compelled him to keep still or cough water. He became grimly, hopelessly calm. There was nowhere to go, nothing to do. What was the point of struggling? The water didn't really seem cold to him any more; the darkness and the confinement were suddenly more reassuring than frightening. Now, far from wanting to panic, he was tempted to fall asleep, to let himself slip down into the water and be washed back down and out on to the path once more. No, it wouldn't work like that. He had to think of what to do.

If Robinson was dead, and the passage was blocked, then he was on his own. He would have to go back the way he had come. Maybe he wasn't dead. By now, if he had waited, he might have forced his way past the obstruction, or been pulled through it by Marie. That's what they were planning. The thought of pushing his way through the black water again, feeling for a dead body, was almost more than he could bear, but he decided to try once more, and that he had better do it before he had time to think about it too much and imagine what it might be like. Don't think. Don't think. Deep breath. Deep breath. One two three and.

Horace pushed himself under the water and dragged himself forward once more. One thousand two thousand three thousand four thousand. It was at about twenty-five that he had hit Robinson the last time. Twelve thousand thirteen thousand fourteen thousand. Then he bumped into something, two large limbs. The shock was so great that he spun round, his mouth opened and he began to choke, breathing in water. His arms flailed outwards, and his head struck a stone wall. He had given up control and had lost even the impulse to save himself. His only awareness was of fear, not as an idea but as the water he was breathing in, the light dancing in his eyes. But behind the fear, weakly, he felt that the limbs were not static, flapping, but actively gripping him, that they were hands, not feet, and that he was being pulled along the tunnel.

It was all wrong, he was going away from the safety of the air, bumping along the water-filled tunnel. Why not just yield to the temptation and stop holding the air, just breathe the water instead and go to sleep? He was pulled round and pushed against stone. He was in air, not water. He began to cough and choke as he was bumped and scraped along. His gasps for breath were blocked by the water in his nose and throat and chest. Suddenly, he was out of the darkness and in unbearable brightness, turned over once more and roughly pushed and squeezed. He coughed and vomited the water out. When this spasm was over, another, different one began. Sharp pains in his chest and stomach bent him double. He sobbed in shouts and struck out in the darkness, then he vomited once more, constricting his stomach again and again until he could expel nothing but gluey bubbles. He was too tired even to cry. He lay panting and dabbed his fingers in the warm sticky puddle in front of where his face rested, one cheek on the grainy cement.

As he lay half dozing, he became conscious of something warm and wet running down his ear and neck, as though blood was oozing out of the side of his head. He turned painfully and bumped his face into a hairy snout. He reached a trembling hand out and rubbed the dog's head. Seamus gave a bark, then stiffened and shook himself, spraying water around him. Horace heard the sound of footsteps, then hands were on him and he was dragged forwards sickeningly, his heels scraping on the ground.

'Sorry about this, Horace.'

Horace, coughing, swooning, could scarcely hear Marie's panting apology. He was set down and lay with his stinging eyes closed. He was sinking into sleep when he felt some sharp slaps against his cheeks.

'Pull yourself together, Horace.' It was Robinson's voice. 'Wake up. Open your eyes.'

Horace sullenly obeyed and saw Robinson's face looking down at him, its expression hidden in the shadow of the grey light coming from above. As his eyes became accustomed to the twilight, he was able to make sense of the scene around him. They were in a cavernous chamber dimly illuminated through an opening far above them, so dimly that the extent of the space could not be seen. Seamus was sniffing around. Robinson had noted Horace's return to full consciousness and moved away into the gloom. Marie was seated just a few feet away, her back against the wall. Her hair was matted, her wet clothes clung to her body, the skin of her face and arms was deathly pale. She looked like a dead body that had been retrieved from the dark water. Catching sight of Horace, she gave a tired smile.

'So that was easy enough, wasn't it?' she said.

Horace began to cry and tremble violently.

'Can we get dry?' he stammered. His teeth were chattering so hard that speaking was painful.

'No problem,' said Robinson, emerging from the dark. His sweatshirt and jeans clung to his body in a wet sheen. He ran his fingers through his long, dark hair, pushing it back off his forehead. 'If you'll just put your boy scout training to good use and light the fire, then we can hang up the clothes over it.'

'I can't light a fire,' Horace wailed. 'You know I can't. You're horrible. What happened? It was awful.'

'It wasn't great,' said Marie. 'Unfortunately, Rob did not manage to swim through the tunnel unaided. He'll have to do it again if he wants to get his certificate.'

'I thought he was dead.'

'I got wedged in. I was flapping around, working on a plan, when Marie turned up and dragged me through by my arm. She almost wrenched it out of its socket.'

'Did I really?' asked Marie. 'I'm extremely sorry I wasn't able to save your life more carefully.'

'Then she went back for you. The fool. She was hurt as well.'

'Where?' asked Horace.

Marie turned towards him and showed the inside of her left arm. Below the elbow there was a long gash, so deep that the layers of skin were visible. It was like a fleshy entrance to her body, red in the centre, pink and white around the edges.

'Robinson took some pulling through,' she said. 'This is the sort of thing that happens when you get involved with a man.'

Robinson gave a grunt.

'I was drowning,' said Horace. 'I was dying. You saved me. Why?'

'I think we're meant to look after you,' said Marie.

'Thank you,' said Horace.

'Don't be stupid,' said Robinson. 'We'd have left you

behind if we could've.'

'It's the worst thing I've ever done,' said Horace.

'You wait.'

'What do we do now?' said Horace. 'Do we climb up to the light?'

'I don't think so,' said Robinson. 'It looks as if we're in the inside of a furnace or something like that. The walls are like porcelain. We can't climb up those. Anyway, I've got a better idea.'

Robinson had a rare gleam of enthusiasm in his expression.

'What sort of idea?' asked Marie suspiciously.

'I'll show you,' said Robinson. 'Let's see what sort of dog Seamus really is.'

He looked around and pulled a short, wooden stick from a pile of rubble. He brandished it at waist height.

'Look at this, Seamus, what do you think?'

Seamus looked round and sniffed and then ran eagerly towards Robinson, his nose following the movement of the stick. As the dog approached, Robinson raised the stick out of reach, and it seemed to act as a magnet, raising Seamus on to his back legs and making him fall backwards and whimper excitedly.

'What a fantastic stick,' said Robinson. 'Do you want it?'

He thumped it twice on the concrete floor, then tossed it into the darkness.

'Fetch, Seamus, fetch.'

With an excited bark, Seamus turned, his paws slipping at first on the hard floor, then scampered after the stick. He vanished from sight. There was a bark, then a howl which suddenly receded, changed in sound, echoed and faded. Marie and Horace leapt to their feet.

'Where has he gone?' asked Marie.

Robinson took a few steps forward. As they drew close to him he stretched out his arms so that they were prevented from stepping past him. He was looking downwards, and they saw that he was standing on the lip of a shaft whose dim course was lost in darkness below.

'He's down there,' said Robinson. 'At the bottom by now, I suppose. That's the problem with dogs. Show them a stick and they stop thinking. And they're no good at flying.'

5. Down

'THIS IS WHAT Horace has landed us with,' said Robinson.

'Where's Seamus?' asked Horace.

Robinson was briskly looking around.

'There's no way out up there,' he said. 'And there are no doors or passages. So we must go down.'

'No, but where's he gone?'

Marie, who had crouched beside Horace looking down into the shaft, turned her face towards him.

'Don't be so silly, Horace.'

'Is he hiding somewhere? You're joking.'

'Of course I'm joking,' said Robinson. 'I'd like to have seen the look on that stupid dog's face when he found himself flying through the air. Don't worry, though, Horace. He probably caught the stick on the way down, if I got the trajectory of the throw right. He was a happy canine when he died.'

Horace sat down, miserably conscious of his heavy, wet clothes itching on his skin.

'You killed our dog. He was our friend.'

'He may have been *your* friend,' said Robinson. 'We didn't ask for him to be brought along. He was a crap dog. He didn't come up with a single idea during the journey. He was no help whatsoever when I got stuck in the tunnel.'

'He was all right,' said Horace. 'You shouldn't have done that. Should he, Marie?'

She laughed.

'You've got to admit that it was quite funny,' she said. 'That earnest scampering of paws and then silence as he tipped over into space. Anyway I don't much like dogs. The slobbering and the shitting and the tongue hanging out like a bit of raw bacon. All that faithfulness and pathetic gratitude. It doesn't mean anything, you know. The bark of a dog is like the squeak of a gate.'

'I liked having him here.'

Robinson wandered over and stood next to Marie, peering down into the void.

'He wasn't even much use when he died,' he said. 'I listened out for a bang or a squelch or whatever but I didn't hear anything. Perhaps the hole goes down for ever, or maybe his body was too soft to make much of a sound. Anyway, it's all the same. We've got to make a start.' He turned to Horace. 'And you'd better pull yourself together. You've seen what we do with stragglers. And anybody who bores us or becomes irritating.'

Horace looked to Marie for some sign of consolation, but she was contemplating the wound on her arm. It was gaping open, like a small jagged mouth, a mesmerizing hole into her body, a fierce red at its centre, specks of sickly yellow around the lips. She licked her fingertips and touched the edges and flinched.

'How do we get down?' asked Horace.

Robinson turned to him with exaggerated attentiveness.

'Seamus tried the quick way, and that didn't work too well. So I reckon we'll climb down the side. And since we're all wet and tired and bad-tempered, and some of us are a bit sentimental about animals, we'll go now.'

As Horace leant over the edge before stepping down, he felt an impulse to throw himself off, as if the darkness were a soft, welcoming fabric to fall into and be caught by. As he moved his head further forward, he suddenly felt a firm hand grabbing him by the collar of his sweatshirt.

'What is especially amusing about Seamus's impetuous, precipitate descent,' said Robinson in his ear, 'is that there seems to be a way down prepared for us.'

Robinson jumped down from the edge on to a platform, apparently made of wrought iron, which was attached to the wall of this colossal brick cylinder. Further along the platform were some steps, also made of iron, which led down and round the wall in a spiral.

'Is it safe?' asked Horace.

'Safer than the alternative. Go. Before I give you a chance to compare the two.'

Horace began to trot down the steps, his left hand sliding down the railing, his right hand touching the wall.

'They don't build them like this any more, do they?' said Robinson, who was never more than a couple of steps behind him. 'This beautifully pointed brickwork, and look at the delicately scrolled decoration on these railings. One finds it rather agreeable, don't you think? But what the fuck's it for? I don't know what you've come up with here, Horace. It looks as if the stairs around a gasometer have been put inside a giant factory chimney.'

'They're here to clean it,' said Horace. 'So you can go up the inside and scrape it clean.'

'You should know. I'll defer to you on that one. We can probably secure a Grade Two listing for this. We can turn it into an industrial heritage centre. And it's undeniably an impressive monument for a tragically terminated Jack Russell.'

'There's a house ahead,' said Marie.

They were in a forest, a dead metal forest.

'How did we get out of the chimney?' asked Horace.

'What chimney?' replied Robinson.

The path wound its way among great steel trunks and fallen branches of scaffolding; an undergrowth of torn sheet-metal, filings, bolts and screws. The three of them walked along it in silence until they reached an area of waste ground. Robinson said that they seemed to be out of the woods, and Horace gave a shout of amazement and pointed, and there really was something worth looking at. On the far side of the clearing was a small house. It was the simplest sort of construction: dark weathered bricks, two windows on the ground floor, two windows on the first floor, grey slate on the roof. There was a chimney and there was smoke coming from it, and it was spitting out flecks of ash as one might spit out stray coffee grounds. There were lights in the windows.

'What do we do?' asked Horace.

'I don't know,' said Robinson. 'I'm not sure I want to meet the sort of lunatic who chooses to live in this shit-hole. I haven't noticed any branches of Sainsbury's along the road.'

'We've got to see,' said Marie firmly. 'The path goes right past the house. If there's anybody there, they must be there for our benefit.'

'Crap,' said Robinson. 'I've seen no benefit arranged for us so far.'

Horace agreed with Marie.

'We have to,' he said. 'We have to see if anybody's there. They might tell us something.'

'Oh fuck it,' said Robinson. 'Do what this idiot boy wants, then.'

The house had no garden, but there was an incongruous picket fence surrounding it. Robinson strode forward and opened the gate, and they walked up the path. He seized the silly little door-knocker (a stylized brass eagle) and gave it a rit-tit-tit. There was a rustle from inside, and a shadow prickled through the frosted glass in the door. It opened, and an old lady was standing before them. She was not at all like the old women Horace knew. She was especially different from his two grandmothers, brisk, earnest women who were more energetic than their children. This was a real old lady. She was very short, slow in her movements, and she smiled as she saw the visitors in her porch. Her grey hair was tied up in a bun, she wore a loose, flowery cotton dress which reached almost to the floor, and a cardigan of a greyly indeterminate colour.

'Good afternoon,' she said with a welcoming smile.

'Is it afternoon?' asked Marie.

'Fancy not knowing that,' said the old lady. 'It is overcast at the moment, but I'm sure we'll have a beautiful evening.'

Robinson gave a grunt. The woman looked from one to the other of the trio, and when she looked at Horace he saw that her eyes were green and slightly askew, so that she seemed to be looking at something in the distance beyond him.

'Won't you come in?'

'We don't want to be any trouble,' said Robinson, not altogether politely.

'Come in,' she replied. 'I know you have far to go but I won't let you go any further without having some tea with me. Perhaps I can help you.'

The woman stepped aside to admit them. Robinson looked at Marie, as if for advice, then shrugged and stepped inside, having to bow his head as he did so. Marie and Horace followed him. They found themselves in a comfortable front room with a sofa and chairs resting on a thick rug. Pictures and old photographs hung on the walls.

'Please sit down,' said the woman.

Robinson was edgily unwilling.

'Whenever I visit a new house, I like to look around,' he said, eyeing the four closed doors that gave off the room. 'It was the only thing I ever liked about house-hunting. You can root around in other people's homes.'

The old woman smiled and shook her head.

'I'm afraid that there's nothing to see. That door leads

to my kitchen. The others are . . . well, just storerooms.'

Robinson lowered himself on to the very edge of a deep armchair. He pulled off the lace antimacassar and began to pick at it. Horace and Marie sat next to each other on the sofa. The woman remained standing.

'You can't see many people around here,' said Robinson.

She walked over to him and took the antimacassar from his hands.

'You're wrong,' she said, replacing it on the chair back and smoothing it out. 'I have many visitors.' She turned to face Horace. 'And now, shall we introduce ourselves?'

Horace realized that he was being called upon to speak.

'I'm Horace,' he said.

The woman raised an eyebrow and looked at his companions. He was meant to say more.

'This is Robinson. And this is Marie.'

'They are your friends?'

'Not really.' Horace felt himself blushing. 'Robinson is my teddy bear. Marie is my doll.'

The woman reached for an apron that was hanging from a hook on one of the doors and began to put it on. She gave Horace a smile that made him feel he had been caught out.

'I'm just an old woman and don't know about things like this,' she said. 'But Robinson doesn't look at all like a teddy bear to me. I've never seen a teddy bear in jeans and a sweatshirt and trainers. He looks like a young man, a rather dirty and dishevelled and unshaven young man.'

'Oh, do I?' said Robinson. 'Well, with respect, I think I look a fuck of a sight better than you'd look if you'd been through what I've been through.'

The woman smiled but otherwise ignored him. She turned to look at Marie.

'Don't you find, Horace, that one of the problems with dolls is that they aren't very satisfactory when you take their clothes off?'

'What do you mean?'

'Oh, you know what I mean,' the woman said. 'But I'm sure that if Marie took her clothes off, she would be satisfactory. Those breasts look real to me, not the Disney kind, the sort with knobbly, brown nipples on the end. I bet that she's got a real vagina, soft and wet, with hair around it, one that opens up.'

'She has,' said Horace. 'I've seen it.'

'For Christ's sake,' said Marie. 'Do you want me to get my knickers off and spread my legs for you all?'

'Tea first,' said the old woman.

'I don't know,' said Robinson. 'I quite like the sound of that leg-spreading.' He shot a glance across at Marie. 'But before any of that, a couple of us are hurt. Do you have plasters and that sort of thing? And Horace looks as if he's been dragged through an underground stream. Can we wash him?'

Horace looked furious, and the woman laughed.

'I'll get you a bowl of water.'

She opened one of the central doors but, before leaving the room, she turned her head.

'Just stay there,' she said, then closed the door behind her.

'A request or a command?' said Robinson. 'Quick,

Horace, look in one of the other rooms.'

'What do you mean? She said . . . '

Robinson hissed and gestured furiously towards the door furthest from the one through which the woman had left. Horace glumly raised himself up and opened the door. The room was unfurnished, bare boards and bare walls. But it was not empty. In the middle of the floor was a pile of toys, for children of every age. There were little rattles and brightly coloured rubber balls, drums, beads, furry bears, clowns, wind-up creatures clutching cymbals, a skipping-rope, picture-books and dolls. Horace closed the door and returned to his seat.

'The dolls had no clothes on,' he said in puzzlement.

'What do you mean?'

'The clothes were gone, and their arms and legs were twisted in strange positions. Like this.'

Horace twisted his elbow behind his head. He was proud of this ability. He could drink a glass of water holding it with his right hand round the back of his head and round the left side of his face. It sounds impossible, but it's true.

'No, I mean, what dolls?'

Horace started to explain what he had seen, but broke off at the sound of the woman's returning footsteps. The woman edged the door open with the steaming china bowl she was carrying. She placed it on a low table.

'Before tea,' she said, 'there is some washing and repair work to be done.'

'I don't need to wash,' said Horace, as he always did. Baths were one thing, but washing, with flannels being

189

forced over the face and neck and behind the ears where nobody can see, was something entirely different.

'Don't be silly,' said the woman with a twinkling sternness. 'Just look at yourself.'

There was a small mirror on the wall, and Horace grumpily walked over to it. He was shocked by what he saw. His face was dirty, striped with dried tears, coated with hardened snot. The skin under his eyes was stained dark. His hair was dry by now but it stood at all angles, the texture of twined rope.

The woman sat next to Marie and examined the wound on her arm. She dipped a corner of cloth into the steaming water and dabbed on the swollen rim. Marie flinched.

'I'm sorry, does it hurt?'

'No, I like it.'

'Good, because this will hurt a little.'

She cleaned the wound along its lips, then squeezed the two sides together with both her hands. Marie gave a slow cry of pain as yellow and red fluid bubbled out. The woman soaked this up in her cloth which was now heavily stained. She dipped it into the water and squeezed it out, turning to Horace.

'Now for you,' she said.

She grabbed the hair at the back of his head firmly in her left hand and then rubbed the warm cloth around his face, behind his ears and on his neck. Horace pulled his face free.

'That will just make me dirtier,' he said.

'No,' she said. 'It won't.'

Her cleaning became gentler. When she was finished,

she tossed the cloth into the water but kept hold of Horace. She pushed his hair off his forehead, her hands softer than he would have expected. Her fingers moved through his hair, then stroked the back of his neck and dipped down under his collar down his spine. He gave a shiver which awoke the woman from her reverie. She looked around.

'I was expecting a dog,' she said.

'The dog didn't make it,' said Robinson. 'But he gave his life for the greater good of the team. He would have wanted it that way.'

The woman smiled. She looked from one to the other of the companions as if she were a dog herself, sniffing out something mysterious and new. She spoke with a laugh, almost flirtatiously.

'You've been looking behind one of my doors. I can tell.'

She pointed her finger and swayed it, a compass needle searching for magnetic north. It came to rest on Horace.

'You,' she said. 'What did you see?'

'Toys,' he said. 'Lots of different kinds, for different aged children.'

'I keep them here for children who may visit me,' she said.

'And yet,' said Robinson, 'you didn't bring them out for young Horace here.'

'We shall see,' said the woman. 'Tea first.'

She picked up the bowl of water.

'You have now looked into one of my rooms, though I told you not to. Please don't do it again. Now I shall fetch tea for you.'

When she had gone, Robinson whispered to Horace and pointed at the next door.

'No,' Horace hissed back. 'She said we mustn't.'

'For fuck's sake, Horace, hurry up. She'll be back in a minute.'

Horace looked at Marie who nodded in confirmation. He shrugged and got up, his legs tingling, approached the second door and opened it. He saw a room, much like the first, except that it contained piles of children's clothes, of varying sizes, arranged in neat piles. There were doll-like romper suits patterned with balloons and clowns, vests, knickers, short trousers, dungarees, pink party dresses. He shut the door and resumed his seat.

'Children's clothes?' said Marie. 'What does she want with them?'

'Perhaps she's trying to tell us something,' said Robinson. 'Perhaps congratulations are in order.'

Horace heard the sound of footsteps approaching in the corridor. There was a bump against the door.

'Could somebody open the door for me?'

Robinson stepped quickly forward and turned the handle. The woman appeared, carrying a tray which she placed on the table by the sofa. There was a teapot, a jug of milk, cups and saucers, a plate of chocolate biscuits and a dark brown cherry and raisin cake of the kind that Horace especially hated, associating it with long Sunday afternoons spent in the company of vaguely connected aunts, shined shoes, desultory conversation and no running about. As soon as she was relieved of the tray, the woman narrowed her eyes and sniffed once more.

'Somebody has been through another door,' she said.

She looked straight at Horace, who found himself unable to meet her gaze.

'How could you, Horace?' she said. 'I told you that it wasn't allowed, and you all agreed.'

It was the worst thing she could have said. Horace found it intolerable to be in the wrong.

'Promise me, Horace,' she said, 'that you won't break your promise again. You won't look into the third room.'

'Why?'

'Because I don't want you to. Come, Horace, you have broken your word twice. Will you do this little thing for me? Well, will you?'

'Yes.'

'Do you promise?'

'Yes, I promise,' said Horace a little impatiently.

'Tell me, then,' she said. 'What did you see?'

He took a deep breath.

'Only children's clothes.'

'For children, of course,' she said. 'For the children who visit me.'

'Pity you didn't offer Horace a change of clothes,' said Robinson. 'He could certainly do with one.'

The woman ignored Robinson.

'You must tell me all about your journey, about the obstacles you faced, your cameraderie and the inevitable little differences. And of course what happened to your dear dog. You must tell me all about it, Horace.'

Horace's face registered alarm.

'First we shall have tea,' said the woman.

Horace reached for a chocolate biscuit, but Robinson leaned forward and urgently gestured him back. He turned to the woman.

'I'd like some sugar in my tea, if that's all right. We could send Horace to get it.'

'No,' said the woman quickly. 'I'll fetch it. You can pour the tea.'

Robinson smiled and watched her go but, as soon as she was out of the room, he leaped forward and pushed the door shut behind her. He gestured to Horace and to the third door.

'I can't,' he protested. 'I promised.'

'Why the fuck do you think she made you promise?' Robinson hissed. 'Get over there, you little cunt.'

Horace giggled. He got up and went to the third door without his previous nervousness. It would just be the same sort of stupid things for children. He opened it. On the wooden floor was a worn laminated steel bath full of heads. For just a moment, Horace thought they might be dolls but, though they were clearly children, apple-cheeked, snub-nosed, large and heavy. They were real. There was no doubting the expressions of dismay; the glazed, dull eyes; the hair with partings combed by someone, or coloured ribbons tied by someone, yet hacked at the neck and piled up. Some stared at Horace with expressions of earnest inquiry; others were upside down and unreadable.

He turned to Robinson and opened his mouth but he could make no sound. His stomach folded up as if he had been winded, and he attempted to vomit, but there was nothing left, and he could only cough and splutter out air in spasms. Robinson and Marie rushed to the doorway and Marie quickly shut the door. At the same time, the door behind them started to open. Robinson threw himself against it to push it shut, but the woman had pushed her hand through and the door closed on her wrist. There was a cry from the other side of the door.

'My hand's caught,' the woman said. 'Please open the door.'

'Pull your hand back,' said Robinson.

'I can't. It's trapped. Open the door, it's hurting terribly.'

The three looked at each other questioningly. Marie pulled a face.

'She's an old woman. We can't just leave her with her hand trapped in the door,' she whispered.

'Oh, can't we?' Robinson whispered back. Then he raised his voice. 'I'm sorry, the door seems to be stuck. I'll try to pull it open a little and you can pull your hand back.'

He leaned forward slightly, allowing the gap to widen. Instead of retreating, the woman's hand reached round the door and clawed at his face, leaving three shining, red furrows on his cheek. Robinson yelled and forced the door tightly against the arm once more, which was now through as far as the elbow.

'Get the knife,' shouted Robinson, pointing at the tray.

Horace looked around. There was a carving knife next to the cake. He handed it to Robinson who shook his head.

'No, you do it. Go for her.'

'I can't.'

'You fool,' said Marie. 'I'll do it.'

She took the knife from Horace by the blade and, visibly puzzled over how best to hold it, seized the handle so that the sharp point was downwards. She raised her hand and brought the knife down hard, with a grunt of effort, into the old woman's arm. There was a great scream from behind the door, different from anything Horace could have expected. Marie pulled the blade out, dripping red.

'Pull your arm back,' Marie shouted.

There was more screaming and whimpering, and the hand was still clawing blindly. Marie was screaming now.

'You'd better fucking pull it back,' she shouted.

There was a heavy thumping at the door as the woman pushed against it with her shoulder.

'Right,' said Marie.

She grabbed the woman's wrist with her left hand and jammed it hard against the wall by the door-frame. Horace saw her begin to saw at the hand. He turned away, but he could hear the scrape of the serrated blade against sinew and bone. The scream from behind the door became a bestial shriek. Marie leapt back, and Horace saw a spray of blood issuing from the mutilated hand. A finger lay like a practical joke on the floor, bone, sinew, bubbling flesh at one end, an improbably pristine nail at the other.

'Fucking pull it back.'

Now the arm was pulled back through the gap, and Robinson slammed the door shut and leaned back against it. The three of them, blood-spattered, panting, trembling, looked at each other.

'Any suggestions?' asked Robinson.

6. Away

FOR A FEW seconds, there was silence, not even a sob, from behind the door. Suddenly, a scraping sound was followed by a heavy collision with the woodwork, then more scraping and another collision, as if a battering-ram were being smashed against it.

'That can't be her,' hissed Marie. 'She couldn't do that.'

Robinson's whole body was wedged against the door, preventing it from being forced open. It was hit again and again.

'What do we do?' asked Horace. 'What do we do?'

'I've got an idea,' said Robinson. 'We've only got seconds. We've got to act quickly. Marie, come here and see if you can hold the door.'

Marie took Robinson's place leaning against the door. There was a blow against it which almost threw her off her feet, but she held firm.

'Can you keep it shut?' said Robinson.

'I think so. For a minute or two, anyway.'

'Good. Come here, Horace.'

Robinson took Horace's hand, led him to the front door and opened it. They looked back at Marie, whose body was flexed tight against the door, her shoes on the wooden floor, held firm by her hands on her knees. With each blow against the door, she flinched. She was breathing in gasps, her face was flushed scarlet, the wound on her arm was beginning to ooze once more.

'Well?' she said.

'If I'd had more time,' said Robinson, 'I might have come up with a proper plan. I'm sorry, Marie. Bye-bye.'

He pulled Horace through the door and slammed it behind them. Before Marie vanished from sight, Horace was able to see her comical expression of surprise. Perhaps she was wondering whether to chance it and run after them. Horace started to think about protesting, but slowly enough for it all to have time to happen, and they were away from the house and there was no going back. They ran like thieves out of the garden and then, after a glance to the left down the path from which they had come, they turned right, where the path wove among heaps of rubble. They ran and ran. There were mingled howls behind them. Was it the wind? Darkness was falling, and it was cold. Icy mist hung in the air. It was like running through clouds.

'Faster,' shouted Robinson, 'we've got to get away.'

The two ran together until Horace's chest began to heave with pain. He stumbled and lost his footing, and Robinson even attempted to drag him for a few more yards until he stopped too and both of them lay on the ground, gasping for air. Horace heard a coughing sound and wondered if Robinson was ill but saw that he was laughing wheezily.

'You look awful, Horace,' he said. 'Too many chips, I suppose. Come on, now. Walk.'

Horace took Robinson's hand, and they followed the path, which seemed now to be winding downwards. It was murky and blustery, the air flecked with spots of rain. Horace could see almost nothing, and his eyes were fixed on his feet as they moved him forward. Robinson began to sing raucously an approximation of a tune that Horace knew well:

'And if one stupid woman shouldaccidentallyget chompedupbysomesortofmonster—there'd be two people le-eft, walking along the path.'

Horace said nothing. Robinson looked down at him.

'What did you think of my plan, Horace?'

'It was horrible.'

He laughed.

'Do you wish that I had left you behind instead of Marie?'

'I couldn't have held the door shut.'

'No, I know.'

'We could have blocked the door with something.'

'Maybe. I didn't see anything to block it with, though. No, I done good, Horace. That situation called for the sort of person who tricks dogs into jumping down bottomless pits just for fun. It was Marie's own fault. I was the one holding the door. She could have just left me there.'

'She thought you had a plan.'

'I did have a plan,' said Robinson. 'It just wasn't very

good from Marie's point of view if what she wanted was not to be dismembered in order to slow the enemy down.'

'You're bad,' said Horace. 'You're a bad person.'

'I'm here,' said Robinson. 'And you're here. And Marie's head is probably a part of the head collection in the tin bath. Did you see the look on Marie's face? It was the only thing that made me want to stay. But if you don't find it funny, then just don't think about it. Don't bore me though. I do unpredictable things when I'm bored with people.'

Horace decided that he would never say anything ever again to Robinson. They continued downwards for several minutes, stumbling occasionally as the path steepened. With no warning, Robinson stopped.

'Do you hear something?'

Horace was stubbornly silent.

'Water,' said Robinson. 'Down there. And it's not an old canal either. I can hear bubbling and rippling. Something's banging as well. It sounds as if somebody's hammering. Let's go. Quietly.'

In just a few minutes they had reached the water's edge. They were on the bank of a river that flowed down to the right, away into the darkness. The path ended in a small, dilapidated jetty. A rowing-boat was tied to the end of it, the current dragging it and swinging it repeatedly against one wooden pillar. Thump thump thump.

'I suppose we get into it,' said Robinson. 'It will make the journey easier, anyway.'

He put one foot on the jetty. A plank creaked.

'You try it, Horace. See if it will take your weight.'

Horace stepped out on to the jetty. It seemed to sway beneath his weight. A few steps took him to the end, and he looked down at the boat. Down on its floor, the two oars lay neatly side by side.

'What do you think, Horace? Is it OK?'

Horace had looked at the rope and seen that the boat was tied to the jetty with two simple knots. He walked casually towards it and began to pull at them as if he was just fidgeting. They seemed loose. He looked towards Robinson.

'There are no oars.'

Robinson looked unconcerned and made as if to join Horace.

'The current will carry us.'

'I think I saw some oars over there, at the bottom of the hill.'

'Where?' asked Robinson. 'Are you sure? I didn't see them.'

'I saw them over there.'

Robinson gave a huff.

'Well, I'll go and have a look then.'

The first knot came away easily enough. Now it would just take a single tug at the rope and it would be free. He looked round. Robinson was far enough away. Horace slipped the rope out of the last knot and pulled it off the post that secured it. Still gripping the rope, he jumped from the jetty down into the boat, lost his footing and fell on to the latticed wooden floor, bumping his forehead hard and bringing tears to his eyes. He could taste blood. The leap had immediately pushed the boat away from the jetty, and when Horace got up and turned round he was already clear. There was a clatter on the jetty and Robinson was there, reaching towards him. Horace was able to see clearly the look of puzzlement on his face.

'Horace,' he called. 'Did you fall over? You can get it on to the bank further down.'

Horace shook his head. He was moving away and he thought he saw a smile on Robinson's face and a gesture of the hands. Was he waving? Shaking his fists? Clapping? This was the last Horace saw of Robinson as the boat, now in the middle of the river, picked up speed in the full force of the current and was carried round the bend and away.

7. Boat and bed

THERE WAS NO need for Horace to think or worry or make plans. He had made a single decision and taken a single action, the leap into the boat, and he was released and carried away. It was unnecessary for him to brood on what he had done, or even to remember it. That was in the past and miles back, upstream. He laid his head down and allowed the boat to carry him along the indifferent river through countries that posed no questions or threats. With eyes half closed against the fierce sunlight, Horace felt himself borne under dense forest, the shadows of branches sweeping over and past, the sun flashing through the leaves and sometimes lost altogether in the thick canopy of extended branches. Motion became time, the trunks ticked off one by one as the boat swept by them, the bubbling of the water on the other side of the hull, an inch from his ear. Yet the boat was immobile as well, Horace realized. It was held fast in the river, and it was the river that was in motion over the land, skimming over its surfaces, restlessly seeking its slopes and fissures.

After a while, Horace sat up and saw himself drifting through rolling green hills which then smoothed themselves out and became flat. The river had widened and fragmented until, winding its way through muddy islands, it no longer looked like a single stream at all. These too became more sparse, the banks receded and the boat was carried out on the tide to the open sea.

Horace could taste the salt in the damp air and he could feel against his thighs the tired green waves slapping the light timbers of his boat and he was carried away out of all sight of land. Horace knew that the sea was not blue. He saw jagged greens woken and scattered into gold by the rising sun and he saw soft, speckled violet receding into grey as it sank back behind him. The skin of the sea could be metallic and impenetrable or, with the sun above him, it could be a mountain of glass and he would stare down through its fathoms at the shadow of his boat on the bottom and of his own shadow projecting out of it and waving at himself. The water could be as smooth as a rippling sheet or it could explode and heave vastly, tipping the tiny boat sickeningly down its vast temporary slopes.

Always eastward, Horace drifted through purple luminous mists, swaying curtains of silver rain, spun round by currents and whirlpools. Sparks danced round the boat's bow, flashes of lightning suspended it against the black-crimson of the waves. He drifted under a roof of stars which were reflected on the still water so that when he stood and looked around, the horizon had vanished and he seemed to be lost in deep space, but a space that was increasingly fetid and warm. The sea became stale and grimy. Horace had felt cleansed by the cold waves, but the air was now clammy, the water itself slow, thickening. The sound against the hull was no longer the lapping of water but the rustle of seaweed, the scraping of marine debris.

Not just the sea but the whole world was coming to a halt, calcifying. The progress of the boat slowed as the water coagulated into a brackish swamp. The sea was heating and decaying and consuming itself. The boat came to a final halt as if grounded on the sand, except that there was no ground. Horace tentatively leaned over the prow and touched the slimy heated surface, then stepped out and set his foot down. He would walk from now on. He turned for a last look at the boat, stranded, as if it had been abandoned long before by a receding tide, and it was now half buried in mud.

Horace turned and walked on. There was not much further to go, and just a few more steps took him to the edge. It really was an edge, at the very end of this world, with just one deep step down out of it on to a narrow shelf and beyond and below that nothing at all. Horace peered over the lip of the edge and saw, without much surprise, that a man was sitting down below. Horace had made no sound, but the man looked up and smiled.

'You got here. Well done,' he said.

'Who are you?' said Horace.

'I'm the gatekeeper,' said the man.

'You don't look like the other one,' said Horace.

This man was young and ruddy complexioned, with

long golden hair in ringlets.

'That was a gate in. This is a way out.'

'It doesn't look like a gate.'

'A door might be a better word for it,' said the man. 'If you go through it from one place to another, then it's a door.'

Horace looked down uncertainly. His toes were projecting slightly over the edge.

'Tell me about your journey,' said the gatekeeper.

'It wasn't what I wanted,' said Horace. 'It wasn't what I thought would happen. I want to go home. I just want to go through the door.'

'Then go through the door,' said the gatekeeper.

'I don't know how to.'

The gatekeeper's smile floated upwards.

'It's easy, Horace. What were you told at the beginning of the journey? Where were you heading?'

'We were . . . I was told to follow a light. But I haven't seen it for ages. We didn't bother about that. We just forgot about it.'

'It's often like that. But look again now.'

Horace looked and there was a light now, but far away, deep and distant.

'I can see a light down there, but what is it?'

'That's home. Or the way home.'

'But I can't get there.'

'I'm here to help you.'

'But I can't get down there.'

'Just jump down from there, and I'll catch you. It's not very far.'

On the brink of the abyss, wild and dark, Horace stood and wondered about what he had left behind and what might be ahead. The gatekeeper stood below him with his arms stretched up in readiness.

'I don't want to,' said Horace.

'There's nothing to be afraid of,' said the gatekeeper. 'Just jump into my arms. There's nothing difficult about it.'

'Will it be all right?'

'Trust me.'

Trying not to think, Horace pushed outward with his legs from the edge and felt himself fall. As soon as he saw that Horace had jumped, the gatekeeper withdrew his hands and stepped aside. Horace gave a scream and saw that he was missing the lower ledge altogether as the momentum of his jump took him out and into empty space, turning over and over like a tumbling leaf. Yet his progress was slow through the thick air, and when he spread his arms out he found he could transform his descent into a curve which then took him in a parabolic turn. As he revolved, licked by the rays of the sun, he could see the huge wall of the world he had left behind him, the stars all around him, and the cold light of home below. Savouring his power and control, he spiralled downwards, and the light grew and spread itself out to meet him, until it seemed he was not falling but was suspended and enveloped in a chilled brightness that over-whelmed him and replaced everything else—the other world, the sun, the stars. Then the light faded, and the cold with it. As Horace sank into darkness, he felt a dot of warmth somewhere in the centre of his chest, pulsing, spreading its heat in waves through his body, along the limbs, until he could feel the pumping even in the tips of his fingers and toes.

Horace began to cough and as he did so he felt himself constrained. He felt the rough surface of a blanket. He was in his own bed and he opened his eyes and saw two large faces peering into his own.

'You fucking idiot, what were you playing at?'

His mother.

'Lori, for God's sake.'

His father.

'You shut up. You stupid fucking idiot, you could have killed yourself.'

Horace smiled happily, and his eyes closed once more. When they opened again he was alone and, though he didn't feel tired, he decided not to make any movement for a very long time. Every fold of the blanket, every crease of the sheet, felt perfect, melting into his own folds and pores. With his head still, he looked out at the solidity of his room restored about him.

The world of Horace's room was metamorphic. The dinosaurs were gone. The reason for their extinction was simply that Horace had become interested in other things. But from his oblique, awkward vantage point Horace could see familiar objects: the trolls with pink hair, the plastic Mickey Mouse, the postcard of the little girl clutching the dove to her flat bosom, the heavy brass second-hand telephone abandoned by Henry and Lori as impractical and donated to Horace, the Aladdin's lamp whose limited repertory of predictions Horace had quickly exhausted, the wooden iron, the tambourine, the remnants of a cardboard castle that had been assembled by Lori during an angry afternoon and early evening and later sacked by aggressive forces coordinated and led by Horace.

The toys had been tossed in the corner, perhaps in the rush to get Horace into the bed. Among them was the crushed teddy bear, its gauzy opaque eyes pointed up at the ceiling; the doll with her head bent impossibly backwards; and the threadbare dog. The eyes were buttons. Horace felt no impulse to bring them into the bed with him. They were just toys.

Part Three

I

IT WAS ALL just awful, an awful day from beginning to end. Of course, the early part no longer seemed important and was forgotten. We'd just had the standard row, which was concluded by me marching out and slamming the door. It felt like a ridiculous, theatrical gesture as I was doing it, and I knew that it was the sort of thing that Henry would never stoop to. He wouldn't do anything as positive or brash as that. He would be more self-conscious about it, ironically and quietly easing the door shut with exaggerated care.

That was all in the past. Horace was now up in bed, and the doctor had come, an Asian man, unshaven, tall, young. As it turned out, there had been nothing for him to do except look disapproving, and he did that with a sort of professional seriousness.

'Mrs Dean?' he had said with a raised eyebrow.

'Muz Gale,' I replied, as I so often have to.

'I'm sorry.' He looked down at a piece of paper. 'You

are Horace's mother?'

'I kept my . . . I kept my own name.'

'Yeah, yeah.'

It's so boring. It's like living in a road with a long name and writing it out for the ten millionth time. It sometimes makes me wish I was Mrs Dean, just the thought that I could have done something productive with the thousands of little bits of my life that I've spent explaining that it's not my name. We were whispering in an embarrassed, comical sort of way, even though we were standing outside Horace's room. He was fast asleep, and ever since he was born he has been completely unrousable. If he's asleep, he won't wake till he's ready, and if he doesn't want to go to sleep, he won't, however long you leave him. We could have talked as loudly as we wanted, but that's not the way you talk with doctors. You've got to strike the appropriate tone.

Henry was downstairs making tea. That was another bit of the way it was done. It didn't have to be tea. He could have been changing a light-bulb or a fuse in the plug or putting new batteries in the electric doorbell, which are the three other things he can do around the house. The point was that the man was somewhere else doing something notionally practical, while the woman came upstairs to weep with the doctor at the door of the sickroom. Henry feels the need to maintain these rituals. When the car has broken down somewhere, and we don't have a clue why it's not working, the RAC man arrives and lifts the bonnet, and Henry has this way of standing at his elbow and murmuring agreement about the manifold or the carburettor or whatever it is, as if this is the sort of thing that men understand, while the lady—me—sits in the car and looks at her reflection in the little mirror that's been considerately placed on the back of the sun shield to stop her moving the rear-view mirror and getting it out of position for the male driver.

We had no choice about calling the doctor. Horace had been some sort of blue colour, for Christ's sake, when Henry found him. But it was clear that there wasn't much for the doctor to do. He had his small bag with him, of course, but all he did was flourish the stethoscope and pull back Horace's eyelids. When I asked what he was actually looking for and whether he'd found it, he just mumbled something incomprehensible.

At the bottom of the stairs, Henry appeared in order to hand Dr Shohan tea in one of our earthenware mugs that are designed to look good on country-style dressers. I hate them, a rough wholemeal texture on the tongue, as if they haven't been cleaned properly. Henry asked if everything was all right.

I almost said something rude. I could clearly see that after being the handyman, Henry was now playing the role of worried father. Henry knew that everything was all right with Horace. He was just trying to demonstrate that he was the trustworthy, unflappable one. But then who was it who had been in the house at the time?

'Do you have sugar?' asked Dr Shohan.

I asked if he wanted to come through to the kitchen, but he shook his head. He had been on several calls already and had more ahead of him, ones where he would speak in earnest, hushed tones to respectful laypersons.

When people ask for sugar in our house, it's a cue for much rooting around in the back of cupboards, the way that it is when I ask for ashtrays in other places. Henry went out to the kitchen and returned with an almost empty bag of caster sugar. The doctor had to scrape at the bottom with his spoon in order to extract a couple of feeble white sprays. He seemed distracted. He took two gulps of tea. He had misjudged the temperature and he coughed. There were drops of tea everywhere. Even the stubble on his face glistened. He dabbed at it with a yellowed tissue from the pocket of his anorak.

'You are very lucky and you have perhaps been foolish. There is no problem with your son. He has suffered no physical harm. He may be upset by his experience. That I cannot say. He may become upset or frightened later. I do not know.'

'There was no problem with lack of oxygen then?' I said.

'Yes, there was a problem. He . . . you also, were lucky. It could have been very serious. But I think that he has no severe ill effects.'

'Thank you so much, doctor,' I said, the way that emotional mothers do at times like this.

Dr Shohan bowed his head, as if he had pulled Horace from the fridge himself and restored him to life.

'I am sure it is all right, but if there is any problem, just call me or bring Horace into the surgery. Thank you for the tea. Goodnight.'

He handed me the tea and began to fiddle with our impossible door. Then he turned back.

'I must tell you that I am compelled to report an incident of this kind. It is a completely routine matter, but you may be visited by a person from the social services department.'

Like an idiot, I asked what for, and then realized and smiled and said of course, as if it was something we all agreed with and were also rather amused by. Henry seemed not to notice, as usual.

'Don't worry,' said Dr Shohan. 'It will not be important. But I do think you should get a new fridge.'

'Why?' said Henry. 'I don't think Horace damaged it.'

'That is not my point,' said Dr Shohan. 'It is not safe to have a fridge which locks as yours does. You should get a new one that can be pushed open from the inside.'

'Still,' said Henry, 'it's a pity to lose that lovely chrome exterior. They knew how to make fridges in those days, didn't they?'

'Your son nearly died in it, Mr George.'

'Mr Dean. I was joking, Dr Shohan.'

'Please let me apologize on behalf of my husband, Dr Shohan,' I said. 'I think he may be suffering from some kind of shock which is provoking unpleasant symptoms.'

Finally, and with obvious relief, Dr Shohan got the door open and stood on the threshold of the world of sanity outside

'Yes, it has been a difficult day for you. Goodnight.'

Predictably, Dr Shohan almost crashed into my mother as he turned to go.

'Is this the doctor?' she asked.

It was an unnecessary question. There could have been

no ambiguity about this man leaving our house with a leather bag in his hand and a bleeper attached to his top pocket. But the question was deliberately unnecessary. Let this occasion not be permitted to pass unmarked by her comment.

'Is it dangerous for a child to be locked in a fridge, doctor?'

With evident irritation, Dr Shohan halted, his feet fidgeting on our truncated, cracked path.

'If the child cannot get out, then it is dangerous, of course.'

'Will Horace recover, doctor?'

'He is fine, Mrs . . . er. He is not ill.'

'Are terrible accidents of this kind rare?'

Dr Shohan shrugged helplessly.

'I am sorry, I do not know.' He tapped his bleeper. 'And I must go now.'

He took out his keys and fiddled awkwardly with the lock of his car, self-conscious under the gaze of the three of us.

'He's clearly a good doctor,' my mother said, as the car drove away.

'There wasn't much for him to do.'

'Well, they say that the test of the really good doctor is not just knowing what to do but knowing what *not* to do.'

'Who says that?'

'Randolph told us. And did you know that his daughter, Celia, has just gone to medical school?'

'Shall we go inside?'

'And it's a good sign that he comes to visit. They don't

do that any more. You know, when I was a girl, my father would be woken up every single night, sometimes two or three times. Everyone in the district just expected him to be there twenty-four hours a day. It ruined his health.'

'He did live to be ninety-two, didn't he?'

'Yes, but you remember the state he was in.'

And so on and so on. The rest of the evening was grisly, and I know that it was basically my fault. Henry was in a completely fucked-up state about it all, and that just made him flippant, which made me angry, though I should have known better, and alienated my mother even more than usual. I was being defensive and cold and refusing to get visibly emotional, which was childish. Mother was being ostentatiously alarmed, which she often is about really trivial things, but in this case, admittedly, there was something to be alarmed about.

It was farcical as well as ghastly. Henry had been in the front room and heard this enormous crash and rushed into the kitchen thinking that the ceiling had collapsed. The fridge had toppled right over and was lying with the door downwards. He then tipped it back and opened the door and found Horace passed out inside it. If Henry hadn't been there to hear it, then that would have been that. It was bad enough my mother asking theatrically earnest questions about 'how could this have happened' and so on. I'm not against talking about things. Quite the opposite. I felt that I needed someone like Sue or Petra to talk to about it but I began to feel resentful that I was having to deal with Henry being hysterically frivolous and my mother's wrinkled forehead of concern and her 'just wanting to get the facts sorted out.' I started to behave in a sulky, adolescent way, and it all went badly. Henry was suddenly not there and had wandered off to bed, and Mother made an awful, dignified exit.

My mother's a therapist, and she looks like one. When cheesecloth finally came back into fashion, she was the great beneficiary. She wears her straight, grey hair tight down on her head and tied in a hard bun at the back. She trained after my younger brother, Chris, took his 'O' levels, and now she listens to people for a living. We sat at the kitchen table with the overhead light shining unsympathetically down on us, the shadows cruelly emphasizing the lines in her face. She looked scared and old. At the same time, it seemed a little indecent when she started trying out her sensitive manner on me. I felt like telling her to keep her therapy for the people who pay for it. In fact, I did say it, in effect, and she took it very badly and stomped off into the night. It probably won't matter much. We're used to little rows. I'm chilly and controlled outside the house, but with family and the people I really know I can be rather Mediterranean in temperament, shouting and carrying on. I throw things at Henry sometimes.

I had come back into the house expecting Henry to apologize. He usually does in the end. He's the one who blinks first. It was obvious straight away that something was wrong. Henry, of course, was hopeless at telling me about it. He spoke about it as if it was some interesting item he'd come across in the newspaper.

'Lori,' he said. 'The oddest thing has happened. I found

Horace in the fridge. He was locked in. He's completely fine. He's asleep in his bed.'

I was brisk and efficient and sprang into action. I called the doctor and felt Horace's forehead and made a hot milk drink to warm him up, but of course he couldn't drink it because he was fast asleep.

I can reconstruct the different bits of what happened, but what seem more important, looking back, are the things I thought about and felt. My mind was set racing. What I really wanted was a cigarette and a drink. I love smoking, lighting each cigarette off the one before, or off of the one before, as my pupils say. I've always loved being the woman who smoked recklessly and drank black coffee and hardly ate anything. I poured three fat fingers of scotch into a chunky glass and sat it on the kitchen table next to a pristine packet of cigarettes and an ashtray. I pulled the cellophane wrapper off the cigarette packet with a snap and sat and read an article in a woman's magazine. 'Oral sex: you know they like it.' Yes, I know they like it. It's just that I don't, though I know I'm supposed to, as some expression of fulfilment, and I've pretended to on occasion, around the time when I was pretending to like beer and opera. I got to see the point of opera in the end, at the stage when I was finally able to admit that I didn't particularly care for swallowing chalky slime, horribly like the watery stuff that you find on top of the yoghurt in the carton, except warm and sticky. I also don't happen to like the idea of this club being jammed into the back of my throat. Occasionally I've heard the whining attempt at negotiation: I do it to you, why can't you etc. etc. etc., but honestly, there's no comparison. Well, there is a comparison, one's like licking the ice-cream, the other's like having the cone pushed down your throat. The article didn't say any of that. It was all, *don't bite* and *if you swallow, he'll be so grateful.*

I switched on the TV and half-followed a discussion between some people in different studios. I put on an old record and listened to one side of it, and then it was suddenly after midnight and the entire packet of cigarettes was finished and I went up to bed. Henry was asleep, and I felt bad that we hadn't talked. We try to have a rule about going to bed at the same time, and when we don't, it's generally a sign that something is wrong. I switched on my bedside lamp and hoped it might wake him up but I knew it wouldn't. He's like Horace. When he's asleep, nothing will wake him. I pulled back the duvet to get in, and it half exposed Henry's thigh, and I pulled it off altogether and looked at my husband's body in the flattering light of the sixty-watt bulb shining through a white lampshade.

Neither of us wore pyjamas, of course. In our whole marriage I had only ever worn a nightie when in hospital, once when giving birth to Horace and another time having an operation. I associated my nightie with the squalor of the public ward, old people wheezing in the middle of the night, curtains round beds behind which unmentionable things were going on. The last time I wore clothes at night was when I was at university. My bedroom was in an extension apparently made of cardboard, and the effect was like sleeping in a garden shed with the door open. I wore a nightie, a vest, knickers, a hat, woollen socks, a shepherd's jumper bought on a Greek island. In the summer, it changed. I shared the bed with Paul, and neither of us wore anything. He has vanished from my life entirely, but the other day somebody told me he had lots of children and was on the board of something. Almost all I can remember of our relationship is him crying in the middle of one night. I can't remember why.

Henry's body is almost hairless, and what hair there is is blond and almost invisible. There are light tufts round his nipples, sparse golden pubic hair, a few sparkling hints of hair down his legs. I grasped his penis and lightly stroked it, but nothing happened. I had tried this before, and it had never worked. Physiologically impossible, perhaps. Henry is thirty-seven years old, and his body is starting to show the signs of it. There are streaks of grey showing in his light, curly hair. Brushstrokes at the corners of his eyes. He is thickset without being solid; he somehow manages to look overweight and malnourished at the same time. He has never looked strong. The new, middle-aged bulge in his tummy is invisible when he is lying down, as he was then, on his back, but the two substantial handfuls of fat around his waist were obtrusive.

The greatest thing I could ever do for any person, the most unequivocal demonstration of love, of commitment of myself and my life, was to have a baby with him, and this was the man with whom I had done it, and there was his sleeping body, and I was conscious that I didn't feel all that much for it. That may show the maturing of a relationship. I remember the evening of our so-called first date, sitting on his sofa, and he made the one decisive action of our entire relationship, reaching across and kissing me. In retrospect, that first promising, expectant kiss seems like the sexual high-point. The sexual returns in a relationship are diminishing, and sometimes at the sad, bitter end you find yourself doing the most extraordinary things trying to capture some of the first excitement. Neither of you enjoy it. You feel a bit ashamed afterwards and sleep back to back and later you split up with all the guilt and regret and go back to being fresh-faced and moderate and virginal with somebody else.

Henry and I haven't reached that stage and we never will. Lying there on the bed he was like an old dog whose smells and farts and drooling you've got used to. You don't feel intensely any more, but maybe if he wasn't there in front of the fire there would be some sense of loss.

I covered Henry again and sat up, my back propped against a pillow. I switched the light off but I wasn't tired. The dark suddenly seemed frightening. I put my arms out. What would it have been like if there were cold close walls there, and I was locked in?

Every month that passes in Horace's life is like a small death, as the stupid little things he used to do drop away and are replaced with more sensible things. I used to love the mistakes as he learned to speak, all the silly habits, the mispronunciations. Sometimes I'd tell them to people, but of course nobody else loves these details the way you do. Bottles were bockles for as long as he used them. For ages he couldn't handle two consonants together, so a train would become a frain and children became fulldren. I thought of taping him but never did. Now he doesn't do it any more. I don't know when he stopped it, but he has, and I can't bear it. Once, after he'd stopped, he came back from his nursery school, and I asked him how it had been, and he said, I fryed and I fryed and I fryed. Which on investigation turned out not to be true. Never trust little children without independent corroboration. If Horace was ever interrogated by a social worker, Henry and I would probably go down for fifteen years.

That's what I did at the end of that awful day. I sat alone, untired in the dark, upright in bed, and I fryed and I fryed and I fryed.

II

THE OTHER DAY we had some people round for dinner. It was the normal sort of thing: lamb, haricots, ratatouille, then zabaglione, all bought and prepared by me after getting back from school, except for the zabaglione which was prepared on the spot. The people were the normal lot as well. There was John and Eloise, whom I've known for ever. There was Val and Garry, whom she's been married to now for almost a year. And Harriet and Tom. They're all friends of mine, of course.

Henry doesn't know anybody, or doesn't see anybody. He is not a self-sufficient person. If only. But for some time, his life had been on hold in hopeful anticipation of the arrival of better things, and one result is the social limbo in which he exists. If I am going to start thinking about who my friends are, then I need to get my address book out and check them out in alphabetical order, or else it's a matter of going through my life chronologically. Thinking almost at random, Sal, who is probably still my best friend, actually went to the same nursery school as I did, and we've been in each other's houses and pockets ever since and we know just everything about each other. It's sometimes almost dismaying. If Paul—that's her husband—knew some of the things about Sal that I know about her, some of the things that I've actually seen, well, he's not a particularly tolerant man. She drives a Volvo now and sends her children to private school (she'd never dream of sending them to the sort of place where I teach) and she doesn't work and all that, but I remember one legendary lost weekend in about 1973 when my parents were away somewhere when we took acid, and she couldn't remember her own name. Really couldn't. I remember her at parties, disappearing upstairs with some boy; once it was literally into the woods with this blond boy she didn't even know. I don't think she ever found out who he actually was. It would sound shameful if we talked about it now, probably, but it was all right at the time, on the whole. You need to do these things to get them over with.

I sometimes play a game in which I imagine people meeting each other at different times of their lives. To take the example of someone that I've already mentioned, Garry apparently goes to church every Sunday. Maybe this wouldn't be a problem for him, and perhaps they've talked it through, but I remember back at college when Val and Beth had a competition to see who could fuck the most people in their year, and Val lost, as far as I remember, only because she thought the field was limited to men. Beth was a typical Lug, as we used to call it, a lesbian until graduation. Now she's married to some accountant, who I'm sure has some buried interesting past, or buried non-interesting past, of his own.

I saw Sue Furst the other day, and she looked great, and there was a virtual crocodile of children behind her, and Guy looks pretty strange but is meant to be terrific. When I knew her, it was all anorexia, nervous breakdowns, drugs. There were people at the time who were in far better shape than her who are now burnt out or even dead. I tend to think that we're all scarred and defined by what we've been through, but there she was, triumphant and unmarked.

I'm aware that this is a major non-insight. What do I expect? We're all in our late thirties now, on the verge of not being able to have children any more. The peculiar thing would be if we were still having one-night stands with boys we hardly know and taking illegal and unreliable drugs supplied to us by dubious characters, often the above-mentioned boys. Perhaps we got it the wrong way round. We should have had the babies in our teens when our bodies were best prepared for it, gained all the additional protection from breast cancer and so on. Then, when the children had left home, i.e., at the age I am now, that would have been the time for the vagrant, anonymous, sleazy sex, with the added advantage that we would be better at it, or at least better able to appreciate it.

The point I was making, though, is that at every stage of my life I've accumulated friends. This isn't entirely a matter of choice. I've discovered—and I'm not saying this as some sort of boast—that I'm the sort of person that people choose to be friends with. Even at school there are colleagues whom I've never had more contact with than running past them on my way to a class, and one day they'll catch me alone and tell me about their depression or their children.

Just last week, Flo Phillips, a sad-looking woman in the remedial department, suddenly said to me over a sandwich during our five-minute lunch break that she wanted to be my friend. It was the right sort of language for the lunch counter. I'd like a coffee and a cheese and tomato sandwich with the tomato taken out and I'd like a friendship. It reminded me of primary school, where when you'd got bored with somebody you simply told them that they weren't your friend any more. They'd probably go off and weep for a bit, but is it any worse than being unavailable for dinner invitations and not phoning back time after time after time until the undesirable couple gets the message?

I maintained this sort of honesty well into my teens, though by then it was probably more of a self-conscious form of sophistication. There were a couple of times when I said to eager little boys, I'm sorry, I should just say at the outset that I'm not going to sleep with you. I was equally frank with the ones I did sleep with. I never let the relationship drift or stagnate. I terminated each one with a brief phone call or a face-to-face dismissal. No apologies, no attempt to soften the blow, just a cool statement that we ought to stop seeing each other. Most people were dumbly acquiescent or simply stunned, but if they attempted to argue, I provided no explanation or elaboration. It was finished, and that was all there was to it.

My mother once actually came out with the advice that

boys wouldn't respect me if I . . . , well, you know . . .
went all the . . . um . . . let myself down. I don't
remember respect being something I much wanted from
the no-hopers and dead-enders that I ran around with. It
was other things. Sometimes it was just fun, that tasted
nice and felt wonderful. I remember at the time sitting in
a classroom and reading some dumb D. H. Lawrence
argument about how the young treated sex just like a
cocktail, and that did make me feel bad because I felt that
sexually I ought to be in touch with the tides and the
movements of the earth. I knew I didn't feel grateful
enough for being supposedly in touch with the moon. My
periods just made me feel awful until I went on the Pill at
some suicidally high dosage.

In June 1982, when I was in my mid-twenties, there was
a sudden fashion for cocktails, and I suddenly reconsidered
the whole thing. I wondered whether there had ever been
anything wrong about sex being like a cocktail occasionally.
You don't want every drink for your entire life to contain a
glacé cherry and bits of pineapple and a miniature paper
sunshade, but sometimes it's what you're in the mood for.

Anyway, the fun was only intermittent. Sometimes it
would be dutiful, like doing homework. You'd be in some
particular setting, or away somewhere, and you didn't
much feel like it but other people were doing it, and the
little boy always wanted to do it, so you just went along
and cooperated, and it was always at the very least interesting in a sordid sort of way. There were times where
somebody would just go on and on and giving in seemed
like the least tiresome way of shutting him up. I must

admit that there were a few times where you'd come back down to the party and the music ('Jean Genie, loves chimney-stacks'—were they really the words?), straightening your dress, or you'd be in bed, trying not to think about the doubtless triumphant, sleeping form lying next to you, and you'd feel that something precious had been withdrawn from your account, but that was stupid, and the feeling soon went away.

There were feelings that didn't fade. There were boys I was in love with in a way that I never could be again. This is the part that I really don't talk about. I found a photograph of Mick Madden the other day, and he actually had sideboards, which now look ridiculous of course, and his hair was like two rows of horse tails hanging in each direction from the centre of his head. His shirt collar looked insane, and the spots on his cheeks were cruelly shown up by the flash. Fortunately, nothing else was visible. I haven't even seen Mick for almost twenty years and I don't particularly want to see him. I think I'm reasonably objective about him as well. If we had made the effort to stay together, it wouldn't have worked. We would just have got bored with each other and drifted apart. But there's nothing in my life that is more real to me than my feelings about Mick.

The Mick I see when I close my eyes is very different from the grinning apparition in the photograph. He was tall and slim with an almost tubercular slimness and he used to dip his head forward and flick back his long hair. He was a combination of my idea of all the poets I was reading at that time, Keats and Shelley and Byron, which is one reason why I never read another poem after I was about sixteen. Poetry was something I grew out of. My longing for him was like an ache inside my chest. The first time we slept together, which was very soon after our first meeting, I had the feeling that my body was literally going to explode. When he first pushed himself inside me, and I slid my fingers over the blue whiteness of the skin on his shoulders, I knew that nothing else mattered and what I was experiencing at that moment could never be taken away from me. I know that I ought to have some bathetic conclusion to this episode, but there isn't one. The actual sex wasn't all that inventive; we were very young—I was sixteen, he was a year older. But none of that mattered. It could never be like that again.

I don't want to be too elegiac about it. I'm glad I had those feelings, and I had them once or twice more in the two or three years after that, but they were something I had to lose. In the end, Mick was not like Byron; he was just a bore with lovely long hair. Even the real Byron wouldn't have worked out in anything but the shortest term. I'm sure he would be funny and beautiful but sooner or later he would have insisted on buggering me and that is something I can't bear to do for anybody. I know that some women say they like it (I've never actually talked to anybody in that sort of detail, though Paula and Chris, to name but two, sometimes insist on talking to me in that vein) and they say that it somehow gives them better orgasms. And I know also that we're all meant to be in favour of experimentation. I've done it a couple of times, in response to repeated applications, and I honestly felt that I was the wrong sort of person to do this. I can imagine it being exciting if I was a strict Catholic or something of that kind and it was extremely forbidden and I felt that I was playing with the prospect of eternal damnation. Henry did it once to me, and I don't think he particularly enjoyed the act as such. I think he was just excited by the idea that he was degrading me in some satanic fashion, and that's fair enough, but it just felt undignified and uncomfortable. If you rubbed enough Vaseline in, you could fuck somebody's nose or ear, but that wouldn't make it enjoyable, and it's not specifically forbidden in the Bible either. When that particular episode was over, and I felt this warm dribble trickling and bubbling out like an unwholesome spring, I asked Henry how would he like it? What would he think if I obtained some six-and-a-half-inch-or-whatever-long dildo, greased it and then shoved it up his arse? His eyes rather lit up at the prospect, and he said something creepily polite like, well, if it would excite you, which I found even more tiresome.

I just don't understand Henry sexually. I *know*, but I don't know *why*. An example. Sometimes when we have sex we talk to each other as a way of exciting each other, though I think it excites Henry more than it does me. The other day, Henry asked me to tell him a sexual fantasy that I'd had, and I couldn't think of anything, so, to stall him, I asked him to tell me one of his fantasies. I thought he might come up with some little idea of being scratched or knocked about or something. In fact, Henry's baroque sexual fantasy involves him being the medical officer at a prison for young female offenders. The detail was copious.

The impudent young women were allowed to wear nothing but loose-fitting smocks to prevent them hiding illicit material, and the principal part of Henry's medical duties consisted of conducting internal body searches which would apparently arouse the subjects, and so on and on. There was more, much more, involving lesbian female warders. At first, I was almost awestruck by the detail of Henry's vision, it was a Sistine Chapel of sleaze, but then I just started laughing helplessly, and Henry lost his erection and got very hurt.

'Can you not imagine what a women's prison is really like?' I said. 'Lots of the prisoners are mentally ill. Your main job would be dealing with pathetic women who had mutilated themselves, or become sick because of a bad diet. And there are drug addicts. There probably are plenty of internal body searches, but I don't think they'd be likely to arouse anybody.'

'It's a fantasy,' Henry said sulkily. 'It's not a White Paper. What's wrong with it?'

I didn't know where to begin. I do believe it's important for us to be honest with each other, but honesty isn't intrinsically wonderful on its own. There is some relevance in what is honestly being said. The other sexual fantasy he saw fit to regale me with was positively alarming. He once said to me that he felt that he now knew how to do sex properly and he sometimes imagined going back to his teenage years and giving each one of those little girls one real orgasm. Yuck. What I object to about this is not just that Henry is displaying the sensibility of a serial killer, but the emotional pedantry involved. He clearly thought that he was being such a man. Really he was just revealing himself once more to be the spotty teenage boy who collects things and organizes them into albums. Let's collect all those bits of the past and arrange them on the shelf in alphabetical order and then tick them off with one orgasm each.

I feel no need to alter my own past, even the non-transcendent bits of it. It wasn't all little aches in the chest. There was lust as well, which isn't the same as the fun I talked about above. There were a few great bestial moments, sweat and slime, sucking and gobbling, grabbing, being fucked really hard, swearing and abusing, and you'd find yourself doing something to some virtual stranger that you hadn't let your real boyfriend do and you didn't feel the pain.

But I don't think that respect came into it very much. The joke was, of course, that our parents mostly didn't have a clue about what was going on. Boys would hang around the house, and Dad would talk to them as if he was a member of the royal family, you know, like, have you come far? And what are you doing at school? And what are your plans? Do you want to go to university? And these boys, who were clever and arrogant and disrespectful, would be embarrassed and edge away, mumbling something. They'd shake themselves with relief when they got out of the room, like a dog that had clambered out of a pond.

There were times when I'd be lying in bed feeling somebody's hair across my stomach, or staring down the single eye of some penis that I can still remember without remembering who it belonged to, and I would think that this was in a different world from where my parents sat on a sofa being 'open' about sex and my mother wanted to be my best friend. I've looked at Horace when he's pressing the buttons on some awful little computer game or sitting in front of the TV and wondered what he'll be able to do that will be inconceivable to me? I've looked at the boys in my classes, five or six years older, all jostling and pumpkin grins. What are they up to? Some are still children who clearly want to stick with their toys. But there must be a few who have discovered that the girls aren't unapproachable at all and are just waiting to be approached and experimented with. They have hobbies. Tim Wilson collects the numbers of trains, Bobby Powell is a thief of rare gifts. Keith Evans pushes his head into a shopping bag lined with glue. Trish Kelly, Dawn Belton and Paula Godwin spend their breaks and lunch-times smoking out by the back gate with boys not from our school, and they're only twelve.

What I should have said to Flo is that I haven't got time to see the friends I already have. My friendships, that collection of leftovers from my past, is like my own private zoo. There's a temptation just to look after your favourite animals of the moment, to spend your time with the tiger, say, or the dik-dik or the penguins, making sure that they're properly groomed and fed. Then I'll have a sudden impulse to go and look at the sloth, whose smell I generally find off-putting, and all I'll find is a lump in the straw at the back of the cage. And there'll be a funny smell from the reptile house, and all the fish will have got mange, or whatever it is that fish get, and the elephant house will be overflowing with shit, and the lion will have got into the zebra paddock and done his food shopping for the next month. No, if you've got an institution like that, then you've got to run it as a whole, and that means clearing out the cages, giving the animals their shots and feeding them properly, and even then there'll be the occasional tragic death.

It's an impossible burden, and it's always occurring to me that Jane's baby was born last summer and I haven't seen it yet and that Kit has just separated and needs help and that we owe the Langs, Phil and Chrissie, Nigel, Andy and Mark and a whole load of others return invitations.

And that's just me, so maybe it's understandable that Henry has no menagerie of any kind, not even a dog or a cat, not even a tortoise which you can put in a box for months at a time. Unless you count Theo, who is a bit like the earthworm that children bring in from the garden occasionally and say that they want to keep as a pet. Henry just has a teddy bear and a couple of stuffed animals and an old doll which he occasionally gets out of the cupboard and knocks the dust off as a reminder of former times.

That's always a sign: when you meet somebody and all you're doing is reminiscing about the old days. That's the moment to bring in the vet with the tranquillizer and put that particular relationship out of its misery. It's even worse with people you've fucked. After it's all over, you go back to chatting about things with them, and then later you go to their weddings and you ask about their children and you get on nodding terms with their wife (and you wonder if she knows about you, and you try and remember something damning but it all fades fast), but the one intense thing between you, the one meaningful connection—even if it's only meaningful because of its meaninglessness, its failure, sometimes its total ghastliness—isn't mentioned.

Then you wonder what the point was of going through all that pain and excitement, and what the meaning was of those experiences that seemed important at the time, or powerfully wrong and forbidden. I've tried to talk to a couple of people about all this—not to Henry, of course—but they didn't quite seem to get the point. It's not a life-is-meaningless misery, which I save for other times, but a what-are-you-left-with quandary. When it's run through your pipe, what are the bits that are left clinging to the inside, clogging it up?

The dinner party was all right. I was sitting at one end and then, going clockwise from my left, were John, Harriet, Garry, Eloise, Henry, Val, Tom and then back to me. From the other end of the table I could hear Eloise, Garry and Val getting into an incredibly complicated and long and tedious argument in which Eloise was maintaining that the really important distinction was not between state and private schools but between opted-out and non-opted-out schools. Henry made some pitiful attempt to draw me into it ('as the only teacher here') but even I couldn't concentrate enough to follow the technicalities of Eloise's argument, though it may have been the amount of Pinot Noir I'd had by that time. (It was a Friday night.)

They're all people who like their discussions. I used to

like them myself. When I was at college, apart from sex and drugs and seminars, my main activity was having amazingly long cut-and-thrust arguments fuelled by instant coffee right through the night. I remember that Eloise would come in, just come into my room without knocking, on her way back from wherever she'd been, whatever the time was, and if I was in bed asleep, she would wake me up and sit on the edge of my bed, smoking. Without my lenses in I'd see nothing but this pulsing, orange star hovering above my duvet. Did I believe in God? What did I think about abortion?

I had one once, but I've never brought that into my discussions. In fact, I've never told anybody about it, not Harriet, who really is my bestest friend in the world, not Henry, and not even Francis, who never knew that there were a few months, shortly after his twenty-first birthday, when he was almost a father. Or actually a father, depending on your point of view. I know that I'm supposed to look back on it with regret. A little bit of me died in that clinic, and all that crap. In fact, it wasn't traumatic in the least. It was just a relief to get it done. It was awful being pregnant, it had completely impossible implications for my life, and I felt pleased and liberated when it was over and get a little impatient when women maunder on about it or, worse, when men start being all sympathetic and sensitive on the issue. But I didn't want it to become some sort of conversational token to be placed on the table whenever the subject of abortion came up. Lori, the woman who didn't get traumatized when she was vacuum-cleaned out, will now do her party piece on the subject.

With people like the collection who were at dinner that night, we've reached a point where we all know too much about each other. All of Eloise's endless arguments derive from the fact that, through circumstances unrelated to her abilities, she's the richest of any us, and her endless diatribes about schools and the future of socialism and the public services are like a cloud of ink that she blows out in order to allow herself to scuttle away behind it. The problem with Tom is that he used to be the brilliant one. People who knew him at school talk about him as a prodigy. He never even took 'A' levels. He just got straight into university a year early. He had a boyish, almost pre-sexual wonderfulness about him at that time which entranced us all. He had blue eyes and this very straight blond hair which dipped down over them. Everything about him marked him out as a shy recluse who wanted to spend his life alone with his work, and this quality attracted women in the most amazing way.

It was a bit like the nativity. Women came from afar and somehow found this boy and they moved in with him and did everything for him. Eloise and I once calculated that during his three years at college he slept with more than a hundred women whom we could name and in the process he showed no interest in them and made no effort with them. That's what seemed to captivate them. Eloise slept with him just to see if there was something weirdly arousing about him, that he had two penises or something. She came round to me the next day and told me that she had found nothing, but that that was the point. The sex was wonderful because it was disengaged and left no mark. Tom had a thin, childish, hairless body and he had shown no interest in his own pleasure, let alone hers. But there was something nice about that. A woman could sleep with Tom knowing there would be no anxiety or failure or jealousy, and after it was over it would barely be remembered.

It's not that things went wrong with Tom; they just stopped happening. He had been a remarkable boy who had done remarkable things. Then he was a remarkable boy who was doing unremarkable things, or not doing anything at all. Gradually, people began to wonder whether his supposed remarkableness oughtn't actually to be a product of the things he had done; if he couldn't do them any more, then maybe he wasn't so remarkable after all. He got a mediocre degree and he met Harriet and they got married and he went and worked for Shell and he did well, but he didn't do *that* well. People didn't tell 'Tom stories' any more, the way they once had, and though Tom hadn't apparently cared at the time, I suspect that he now cared very much indeed. He had a slightly embarrassing fervency, when he started arguing over unimportant things. I sometimes wanted to say to him that we were all old friends, that we had passed the stage of making an effort to interest each other, we were now like trees that had been growing next to each other for years, stuck with each other in the same landscape.

The thing about John, or at least my own private theory about him, is that he's in love with me and always has been. He's the sort of boy I went out with at school quite a lot. He's got that tousled brown hair, and he's fun but with a slightly shy manner and just a hint of internal suffering but not so much that it's going to get boring. We've never had an affair, or even got close, or even got close to hinting that there might be any sort of attraction. (Deep breath, I have actually once been unfaithful to Henry, and I'm not going to go into it too much because it simply isn't important. It wasn't an affair, or anything approximating one. Suffice to say that I was at a conference, and it really is incredible the sex that goes on at those things. People were pairing off all over the place, and the simple fact is that I slept with the deputy head of an innovative comprehensive school in Gloucester. I'm at a loss as to why I did it. I ought to be able to say that we were both incredibly drunk or that we were irresistibly attracted to each other, but it was nothing like that. I've had a couple of moments of real temptation, and this wasn't one of them. Other people were doing it, and I did it as well. Perhaps I wanted to commit adultery just once to see what it was like. The sex was nondescript, but I felt genuinely awful afterwards, worst ever, not because of some twisted idealism, but because I had done it without really wanting to and I had placed myself thoroughly in the wrong and I didn't like it. Anyway, I'll never see the man again, nothing will come of it, Henry will never know, so that's that. It's as if it had never happened. It irritates me, though. In some scheme of things or other that I can't quite forget about, I remain in the wrong.) But I sense that everything that John says when we're all together is in some way aimed at me, to impress me, to amuse me, to make me love him back.

Does anybody actually *mind* someone else being in

love with them? I suppose it becomes a trial if they are importunate and create scenes and pester you. But John is ideal: just dumbly adoring. Sometimes, I feel that I could shut my eyes and warm myself under his gaze, as if it were a sun-lamp.

We've all accumulated too much. Our hulls are so encrusted with barnacles that we can barely get through the water any more. We've ground to a halt in the shallows, and none of us is admitting it. In fact, everyone except me would probably deny it. I know from hints I've dropped that Eloise would say that *we* have all been changed by her money, and that if some of her views have changed, then it is just because she has grown older like the rest of us. Tom has never admitted to any sort of failure, ever, at any stage of his life. I would say that that is a part of his problem but to him his attitude might look like contentment. His huge talent has let him be successful in a low gear. After all, he could have been like the legendary Art Sinclair, who got his fellowship at twenty-four or something ridiculous and then spent ten years on the great masterpiece that we all heard about incessantly and then it finally came out and it didn't seem to be anything so special. I can imagine Tom back then, in bed with some blonde doxy, deciding that he wouldn't take the risk of failing at a high level. He probably knew that in the end he wasn't that good, so what was the point of fucking up his life?

As for John, he would probably deny that he was in love with me at all. Perhaps he's just got a squint and that's what accounts for those intense looks. I sometimes wonder whether my own unwanted skill in eliciting confidences is because I so often forget to put my contact lenses in and of course I would rather have my retinas operated on by hand and without an anaesthetic than wear spectacles in public. So I narrow my eyes and make intense efforts to recognize people whose faces are more than eighteen inches away from my eyeballs and this strained peering, and the watering of the eyeballs that goes with it, could conceivably be mistaken for intense empathy.

I don't especially care for zabaglione, a sort of sickly adult baby food when you come down to it, but it's so noisily effortful while being at the same time so contemptibly easy that I do it occasionally to raise some easy applause from the guests. While I was whipping away at the bowl in the saucepan, I looked at the faces made dramatic and conspiratorial by the candlelight and felt a touch of proprietorial pride. I'd invited these people over and given them food, and now this organism I'd created had taken on a life of its own, though admittedly in the shape of another apparently endless argument, this time about *The Piano*. Harriet was apologizing to Garry and saying that it was a film that women in particular strongly responded to; and John was saying something very hostile about it 'with respect'; and Henry was taking no part in the discussion because when we went to see it he had fallen asleep almost as soon as the lights went down ('I remember something on a beach'), had been woken up by the distinctive shimmer of bare flesh to which even his closed eyelids are apparently sensitive, and then slept again for the rest of it.

Maybe we'd all ended up with the wrong people.

Perhaps everyone would have been better off if they had ended up with the previous person they had been with. As I looked round the table making the adjustment in my head, it all seemed rather plausible. John had lived with Melanie for two years before he met Eloise, and I always thought they had split up just because he wanted to make a symbolic break with his time at college. Then he began going out with Eloise ridiculously quickly, mainly, we all thought, because he couldn't imagine the idea of living alone. Eloise had been with an American student called Christian who had had to go back to the States, and Eloise wrote him a goodbye letter when she got together with John. I've always wanted to meet him again, he was a lovely man. I heard he died, but that may not be true.

Before meeting Garry, Val had had a series of encounters of which I can only remember fragments. A speech impediment; someone unbelievably old; a Lord, or at least a sort of a Lord; a poet. None of those really counts, but before that she lived with Martin Fraser, whom I was at school with, and everybody thought that they would get married, but then one day he told her not just that he wanted to leave her but that he was about to get married to this girl none of us knew who was already pregnant. That child must be about fourteen by now. I don't know much about Garry except that when he met Val he was married and had a child. We stay away from this area of huge interest.

Tom, of course, had had no separately identifiable relationship of note before. Harriet just happened to be the one he was in bed with when the music stopped. Any other member of his harem would have done just as well. I didn't know Harriet until she met Tom. She was only nineteen at a time when we were all twenty-two. I thought she was the most beautiful woman I'd ever actually met face to face. It's hard to see that now, when I know her so well, but I used to wonder whether she had settled down too early. She spent the whole of her time at college coming down to London to stay with Tom, which seemed a bit of a waste. She works as a journalist, and I know that years ago she had a long affair with someone in the office (she told me about it, needless to say), but it ended, and now she and Tom have got two children, and she says that they're happy. I wonder if Tom ever knew about it. Perhaps he doesn't care.

Then there's Henry. It's difficult to imagine, but he was engaged to someone else when we began our affair. She was apparently quite shy and just drifted out of the picture when she saw what was happening. Henry always talked of her as if she was hopeless. The Henry I fell in love with was the Henry who was associated with Deanne. I sometimes wonder whether I prefer that Henry to the one who lives with Lori. I wasn't with anybody when I met Henry. I had been living for two years with a man called Jeffrey, a university lecturer (in engineering). One day, he just said that he wanted us to split up. He had no explanation of any kind. I still don't know whether it was something that I did, whether he was tired of me, whether there was something I could have done to forestall it or persuade him he was wrong. You like to feel that you're in control of your life, but that grinding of gears is still a mystery. And I have to face up to it: if instead of throwing me out he had asked me to marry him, then I would have married him.

We may have lost out because of a slowness of reaction. When something went wrong in our lives, it showed that what we really wanted to do was get married and have children. What we wanted to do was to marry the person before and have slightly different children. There would be none of the little Jacks, Poppys, Pauls, Patricks, Sallys or Horace. Or rather there would be the names but different children, and, if I had my say, nobody called Horace at all.

'Pudding's ready. And there are special sponge biscuits to dip into it.'

III

I'M NOT REALLY a beautiful woman in any plausible sense. I've got slightly mongoloid features—prominent cheekbones on a face that looks as if it has been pushed against a wall and slightly flattened. I also have, in a way that's difficult to explain unless you can actually see it, thin, transparent skin of a whiteness that sometimes drifts into blue. I imagine that if I died and wasn't cremated but put out for the birds to peck at until all my flesh had been eaten or had rotted away, then the skull wouldn't be all that much of a change from the way I look now. I have curly, dark hair of the sort that's referred to on shampoo bottles as normal/greasy, though I'm just as happy using washing-up liquid. I even used carpet cleaner in one emergency, and it seemed to have much the same result as anything else.

I've never bothered very much with clothes or with make-up. I have worn occasional dresses with intermittent enthusiasm: cheesecloth kaftans; floral tents in the seventies; a small black dress in the eighties, which is the article of clothing I was built for; a few sober things which I wear to school nowadays which the boys try to look up, the poor fools. The only beauty routine I follow is to wash every day, except for my face, which I never do anything to at all. It has always been fine. The other girls at school didn't look up to me especially, but then they didn't get jealous of me either. I wasn't the cleverest in the class but I often did better than the girls who *were* the cleverest while they were having breakdowns or were out in the lavatories with their fingers down their throats. And it was fine with boys; I was probably lucky there because I had two brothers and knew that men weren't worth dressing up too much for. Just being able to talk to them without standing in a group of girls and giggling gave me a two-year start on most of my friends. Also, though I wasn't ever especially pretty, I've always had a sexual attractiveness.

The quality that I valued most of all was spontaneity. For years, I found it difficult to understand why people worried about things so much and took so much time over them. Get up, throw your nightie on the floor, pull on jeans, eat cereal, go to school. (I'm talking about the sixth form now. In earlier years, the third item would have been 'pull ridiculous grey dress over head'.) Schoolwork was mechanical and easy. Social life had its emotional demands but it wasn't that bad, and in the end, whatever the awful mistake or capitulation or rejection, you could always go back to your bedroom and shut the door and find that somebody had put your nightie back under your pillow, and so the circle of life would begin again.

I thought I was anarchic because I went wild every so often. I envied Denny who walked out on her family when she was sixteen and went and lived in a squat. Denny was about five feet eleven inches tall, she had long black hair in natural ringlets which always looked as if it had been tossed back impetuously, the skin of her face was very soft and childlike and she had grey, really almost colourless, eyes. When she was out of school, she always wore an Afghan coat, she smoked almost all the time and drank black coffee. In the squat, she actually shared a bed every night with this much older man who was a heroin addict, and she was just in every way as enviable as hell. There was nothing of that sixties virgin attractiveness. She was large, with really big breasts, completely different from me in every way.

Denny was the only person I've ever met where there was no pretence at all; no censorship seemed to operate between her brain and her mouth. She would wander round and pick things up and play with them or examine them. If she felt hungry, she wouldn't stop and prepare food. She would just grab a carrot or an apple and nibble at it without looking at it. When she left home, it wasn't to make any sort of point or to impress anybody. However strange it might have seemed, everything she did had a lucid logic about it that you couldn't argue with, and when she explained her actions, you had to agree with her. She had a complete purity as well. In another world, I could have imagined her becoming a nun, because what else can you do if you are a believer? Running away to live in a squat was living out the worst fears of our parents, an act of wild rebellion, but Denny had some reason for it which made it seem inescapably the sensible thing to do. I can't remember what it was; her reasoning was only convincing when she was telling you about it. By the time you were out of the room, you couldn't quite remember how it had gone.

I still see Denny occasionally, but never really to talk. We nod across rooms at each other but in the last ten years we probably haven't had more than a couple of minutes of head to head conversation. She's a solicitor now, but she's always unpredictable. If I'd known that was what she'd do, I would have guessed that she'd be representing radicals or the homeless, but it's not like that at all. She's a partner in some amazingly grand City firm which does things I don't understand for the sort of companies I've never heard of. She must make an awful lot of money. She dresses very expensively. This doesn't change my view of her at all. It only seems out of character because I've been out of touch with her. I know that if we had been seeing each other and she had talked to me about things as they happened, then every step would have seemed unanswerably logical.

What I remember most about Denny is a talk we once had at the end of a party. I was sitting with her at the table where all the drinks had been. It was that time of the evening when all the beer and the drinkable wine have gone, and the cartons of orange juice, and there's nothing left except for a bottle of warm sweet white wine and some funny egg-yolky drink that you don't quite know quite how to approach. Somebody was sitting by the stereo drunkenly playing 'Sylvia' by Focus over and over again. Denny wasn't maudlin or anything. She wasn't the sort of person you'd sit with at the end of a party complaining about life and being weepy. We were smoking cigarettes, and I was talking to her about life in a squat, saying it was the sort of place I would want to live. I was talking as I might have talked ten years earlier about running away with the circus, packing my rucksack with some sandwiches and my teddy bear.

She didn't answer me directly. She just tapped the ash off her cigarette into a glass. She was a seriously good smoker. More than anybody else, she taught me how to do it with aplomb. Most of my friends held their cigarettes like shop-girls on an outing. They had this awful way of leaning forward to have their cigarettes lit, with their mouths forming a tight little O, and they held them stiffly between their straight second and third fingers as if they had been taught how to look genteel. They were trying to smoke the way that actresses smoked in nightclubs in old movies. But Denny was good at all the different bits: taking the cigarette out of the packet, putting it in her mouth. Whenever I even think of giving up or just cutting down, I can close my eyes and imagine her lighting the cigarette, blowing out the match and then not having to look ignominiously around for somewhere to put it. She didn't fiddle nervously with the match or use the lit cigarette as an assertive instrument when it wasn't in her mouth. The most effective way had been worked out, and there was nothing more to think about.

Then she would speak. She had this habit of not exactly replying to what you said but saying something in a different way altogether.

On this occasion, she said, 'The problem with a commune is that you can't turn anybody away.'

I probably responded with the claim that property is theft, but her epigram about life in the squat stuck in my mind. I used to think of myself as a raffish, bohemian sort of creature whose home was wherever she laid her Afghan coat. It took me years to discover for myself how untrue that was. When I went to Blackbush to see Dylan with nothing except a spare pair of knickers in my shoulder-bag, and the queues for the ladies' bogs were a little Woodstock of their own, I had the sense that I felt something but I wasn't quite sure what. I only realized what it was on the train back, when the insides of my jeans and my shirt felt as if they had been lightly dabbed with jam. The feeling was that I hated this and that I never wanted to do anything like it again for the rest of my life.

So here I am. This is the rest of my life and indeed, as planned, it isn't like that at all. And that's fine, that's how it's meant to be. The other Saturday, Henry had taken Horace out on one of their bonding excursions, and I was sitting in the kitchen having coffee with my mother. Suddenly, apropos of nothing, she leaned across, put her hand on mine, which was awkward because I was holding the coffee mug with it, and made deliberate eye contact. It's a sort of professional tool that she has started to use ever since she began working.

'Tell me, Lori,' she said, 'is everything all right? With you and Henry I mean.'

Of course I put an immediate stop to that. Other people confide in me. I don't confide in other people. But I know the sort of thing she's talking about. Even from the outside there are flecks and oddities in our marriage that must look like problems. I've never considered leaving Henry but, to use his own ridiculous terminology, the thought of leaving him has floated through my mind, and has been prodded and looked at during its progress. There are so many things wrong with our situation, I sometimes think I should have a special form designed to enumerate them to insert in my Filofax: Unsatisfactory things about Henry. They sound tawdry and unsympathetic and trivial when I talk about them, which I never do except to Henry, but they also make me feel a sudden solidarity with all those women in history who were labelled scolds and shrews and had special devices inserted over their head with a flap to restrain the tongue.

I don't blame Henry for being unemployed and I almost don't blame him for the condition of paralysis that has gone along with it. There was always something a bit freakish about the relative success he was going through in the early years of the marriage, and I had a feeling it wouldn't last. I remember when I saw his storyboard for the power shower campaign, which was copied shot for shot from the shower scene in *Psycho,* that I felt that he wasn't a natural salesman. I can put up with that, and when I come back from school and he's sitting on the floor with Horace playing chess or something, then I suppose that's very good. I envy him for that. If the bed had been made, or at least the duvet had been pulled straight a little; if the washing and ironing had been done; if he had been shopping; if the vacuum cleaner had been taken out of the cupboard and given a little walk; if there was some evidence of intellectual activity concerning any-thing apart from the crossword: then I would feel better about it.

It may well be that I'm witnessing a man in the course of a nervous breakdown, and God knows he's got reason enough to have one. Perhaps I'll get up one morning and find his body in a bath of red water and I'll blame myself for ever for not having done something to help him. But I *have* done something. I've earned the money and I've done all the work at home as well. I, and my parents a bit, have provided a space in which Henry can afford to be ineffectual and have a nervous breakdown.

The problems that exist—for me—in our marriage don't involve violence or infidelity or estrangement. Just boredom, familiarity, a cycle of repetition and pre-dictability. Years ago, when I was first trying to teach Horace about numbers, I showed him groups of things arranged, for example, in threes—that was probably his age at the time. When a child first sees these groups, he can't separate the idea of the number from the thing that he is seeing. If you ask him what it is that a group of three oranges has in common with a group of three pencils, he doesn't know what you are talking about. My idea was that Horace would look at three cups, three balls, three dolls, three cars, three biscuits, and that after a while the idea of threeness would abstract itself from them, and he would start to see a number as something that was separate from any manifestation of that number in the world of experience. It didn't work, of course. Horace stubbornly resisted the intellectual leap, and a few months or a year later, it just happened, like puberty. There he was, counting and comparing things, and the number three had become an idea separate from all the mess of real life.

Henry has become an abstract number to me, separate from anything that he does or says. I remember when we first met and we would lie in bed and tell each other things about our lives. Henry would do something and it would give me a new glimpse of what he was like; each new event, almost any statement, would be a development in my picture of him. Now he's just there, like the weather, the greyness in the air. The abstraction of numbers is what gives them their power and excitement. When God created the universe, there were a few things that were optional. He could have decided to give feet to fish, if he had wanted, or given dogs feathers. But 496 is the sum of its proper divisors in any universe or any non-universe, whether God wanted it or not. That's beautiful. The same can't be said for the abstraction of Henry. Sometimes, when I'm feeling bleak, he can seem like the incarnation of every quality that I fear: irresponsibility, short-termism, irrationalism, cynicism, habit, inertia, pessimism, fatalism, nihilism.

Sometimes he's all too specific. A day or two ago I was, as usual, transferring some of Henry's books from the bedroom floor to a shelf, when I started flicking through one of them. It was *The Collected Poems and Plays of T. S. Eliot* and it had a pretentious little note at the beginning from his big love when he was in the sixth form, accompanied by a poem which was doubtless an original composition by the deluded little tart herself. I was looking through the book, not at the poems themselves, of course, but at Henry's little pencilled notes, written, I suppose, when he was at university. I came to 'The Waste Land', which is T. S. Eliot's longest poem, and, from my brief look at it, incomprehensible, and I saw that on the blank page before it began, young Henry had written: 'Not essentially DIFFICULT'. And I thought, Wanker. And after that, I thought, there is Henry, sitting in a room in a university city, writing that 'The Waste Land' isn't difficult and thinking that something has been achieved, while outside, the rest of the world remains unimpressed and carries on with people bringing up families and inventing things and making things. I'm sure he's up in his room at this moment, proving something else to his own satisfaction.

What mother wouldn't pick up her son and walk out on that? The resulting scenario is easy enough to imagine. One day, having arranged for Horace to be round at my mother's, I'd sit down with Henry and tell him that I had decided that he ought to move out. I would give my unanswerable reasons: that his depression and immobility were damaging all of us, and that it seemed that our relationship was contributing to his failure to get his life going. He needed a kick-start, and from this point of view our separation would be a good thing for him. We'd find him a flat, and I'd help with the rent, and then we would both start seeing other people. I would meet someone dynamic and successful and rich. Life would become a progression once more, rather than a desperate attempt to repair the present.

Is that how people work out their lives? I have an image of therapeutically healthy husbands and wives solemnly weighing up the possibilities and coming to rational decisions based on the evidence. We always have to pretend that we're not just taking a chance and we must try not to think too much of all the other possibilities. The new non-linear mathematics came too late for me, and I'm too stupid to follow the little of it I've looked at, but I know what emerges from it. The most powerful computer in the world could only make a guess at the result of a race between two raindrops down a window-pane.

In other words, I'm not going to set off in pursuit of the maximum possible happiness for me and my firstborn. I wouldn't know how to set about it and I wouldn't recognize it if I found it. My only plan is to stick stoically by previously made decisions, do as little work as possible, try to keep the flat reasonably well organized and keep cajoling Henry in the hope of slowing the rate of deceleration a little. Maybe not too much. I've sometimes wondered whether his stolid, relentless, numbed failure of the last couple of years might not be a good thing for us. Late at night, I've occasionally tried to imagine what a successful Henry would be like, what would happen if Steven Spielberg had a brain haemorrhage leaving him with an urgent desire to make a film version of Henry's journey round the Arctic Circle, or if Andrew Lloyd Webber decided to make a musical about Henry's world history of shit. People would be taking Henry out to lunch and asking him to appear on panel discussions. If he cheered up and bought a new suit, he would look quite nice and he would have an affair with some young TV researcher. I would never, ever, leave Henry, whatever happened, however much of a failure he was, even if I found bits of rent boys decaying in his study. Henry is different. If he was feeling a bit more successful and he met a girl who was young and good looking and bright and flattered him and who would do anything in bed, then Henry would leave me. I don't think he'd find it that much of a problem. I'm different. It's not that I'm morally better or anything like that. I just stick to things. When I make a decision, I'm like that elephant in one of Horace's old children's books, I'm faithful one hundred per cent. So it's probably lucky that I'm the successful one, and if Henry keeps coming up with ideas of the calibre of his journey inside the underground pipe that constitutes the River Fleet, then it will stay that way.

When I was growing up, I did, I must admit, have fantasies about what adult life could be like. I'm occasionally distressed by what it *is* like, our chafing against each other, our fearfulness, the lowness of our expectations for each other. On the other hand, some of the fears I once had don't seem so important any more. Death, for example. The idea of physical extinction used to make me want to vomit whenever I thought about it. Nowadays I comfort myself that if Chris Vaughan, our headmaster, and Nicky

Hamilton, who did much worse than me at school and is now far more successful and much richer, and Mal Kennedy, the very idea of whom always makes me shiver with rage, will, in a hundred years' time, all have died, possibly in great pain, then my own dissolution seems a small price to pay.

And Horace will be there, my peep-hole to immortality, my message in a bottle to the future. He's already a mystery to me, has been ever since he was first left at the nursery school when he was three. He quickly developed an all-purpose cover story. What had he done today? 'I played and I played and I played and I played,' he would say. It sounded sarcastic. I just want things for him that Henry and I seem to have given up on for ourselves. Not *thing* things. I mean kinds of freedom, from anxiety, and kinds of trust. What else are children for if you can't project the solutions to your own problems on to them?

IV

'I'D LIKE TO come along with you today,' I said.

We were sitting around the breakfast table. Henry and Horace looked at each other, like bureaucrats considering an application received after the closing date.

'Is that all right?' I asked.

'We're going to the British Museum,' said Henry, as if this were something that would discourage stupid little Lori from going.

'Good,' I said. 'I haven't been there for years.'

'We're going to walk there.'

'What the fuck for?'

'We've decided,' said Horace.

'Like Karl Marx,' said Henry.

'But he lived in Soho, didn't he? That's only about two minutes.'

'In reverse.'

'Don't tell me, I don't want to know. I'm coming along. I'll make some sandwiches while you clear the table.'

Henry apologized to me as he came through with the bowls and plates. It wasn't that he didn't want me to go with them, he said. He very much did. It was just that, quite unfairly and arbitrarily, he had had this image in his mind of Horace and him going together, and for some psychological reason it was always a little disturbing to have to alter this.

'Like the other day,' he said, 'when you came back and I'd eaten the last couple of biscuits that you'd been mentally preparing to eat with your coffee.'

'You mean the time you finished off the entire packet like a pig?'

'That's exactly what I mean.'

Horace was mollified by the new possibility of a picnic, and it was assembled according to his precise instructions. White bread with peanut butter and sweaty processed ham from a plastic packet. A Penguin. An apple and a carrot. Two cartons of high-sugar squash. I carried the picnic in a plastic shopping bag, and Henry carried the umbrella which he said, as he always said, would be an infallible protection against the possibility of rain. The walk was long but almost geometrically simple. Down Willow Road to South End Green where I looked hopefully for a 24 bus. Along Fleet Road.

'It must run under here, mustn't it?' said Henry stubbornly.

'Perhaps we should be walking to the British Museum on the subterranean route along its banks.'

The length of Malden Road, then left past where the market was getting going. I looked at it longingly. But I wasn't even able to raise the possibility. Horace, whom I had previously thought of as the most reluctant of walkers, was striding ahead. Henry and I looked at each other.

'He's been practising,' said Henry in mock disapproval.

In bleak Camden High Street, where we were struggling against the crowd, Henry was proved wrong, and all three of us tried to crowd under the umbrella, which had come free with some insurance policy. Horace was just about all right, low down in the centre, but the umbrella only channelled the water all the more effectively down on to our coats.

'What I meant,' said Henry incomprehensibly, 'was not Karl Marx walking to the Reading Room of the British Museum, but the expedition that Karl Marx and his family and various agitators used to make each Sunday all the way from Dean Street to Hampstead Heath, on foot. Carrying a hamper, not just a Sainsbury's bag with sandwiches for one. They used to take roast veal and tea and bread and cheese.'

'Where did they get the tea?'

'I don't know. Perhaps they had a flask. And they pitched a tent there and played games and read the Sunday papers. They even rode donkeys once. Even Karl Marx himself. Can you imagine him trundling along on a donkey?'

'I didn't know you knew so much about Karl Marx.'

'I've just been reading about him.'

'Well, trust you to get into a real growth area at the very beginning, Henry,' I said. 'Why don't you write a book about Karl Marx now that his stock is so high and he is so influential?'

'He was, though. He sacrificed his own life, and his ideas took over the world.'

'Not just his own life but his family's as well.'

'I know. His children died. His wife lived in complete poverty. Then he got their servant pregnant. But when his wife died, he died too, effectively. Their lives were wretched, and his philosophy is now completely finished. But it was a happy story in a way.'

'Well, write it, dear Henry, dear Henry.'

By the time we reached Hampstead Road, the rain had stopped, and the walk didn't seem so long after all.

'How long is it to the British Museum?' said Horace.

'From our home it's about three or four miles,' I said.

'How far is it from here?'

'About a mile.'

'Could you walk a hundred miles?'

'Henry and I and you once walked eighteen miles in a day, but you were only a baby, and he was carrying you in a sling. That was about enough.'

There was a pause.

'That's seventy-two miles less than a hundred.'

'Eighty-two. But that was a very good guess.'

'No, seventy-two.'

'Shut up, Horace.'

There was a bit of dispute about where to turn left off Tottenham Court Road, and we did it too early and ended up somewhere in Bloomsbury. After some guidance from tourists with maps, we found it and then walked all around it to the main entrance. As our picnic bag was searched, Henry said how wonderful it was that something like this was still free. I said I thought it would be better if there was an admission charge, and he said that it already belonged to us, and I said what about all the tourists? and he sulked for a while but then he cheered up when we got to the Rosetta Stone.

'Can you see anything strange about it?'

'Yes,' said Horace.

'Well, what is it?'

'I'm just thinking.'

'You see,' said Henry, 'there are three different kinds of writing on it.'

'I could see that,' said Horace, 'I was just about to say that.'

'The point is that they say the same thing. It was from this stone that they learned how to read Egyptian writing. That picture writing there. It's called hieroglyphics.'

'I knew it was called that. You didn't have to tell me.'

A white-haired old woman had been observing Henry and now came up and spoke:

'Bless you, young man,' she said. She was American. 'Bless you. I think it's wonderful to see a father educating his son like that.'

'Oh well,' said Henry.

'Don't be modest,' she said with energy. 'It's a wonderful thing.'

She moved away, still singing Henry's praises to her companion.

'You're blushing,' I said.

'I ought to marry her,' said Henry. 'She appreciates me.'

'Now there's a project that could earn you some money. She's probably quite well off.'

'She'd probably be sexually appreciative as well.'

We drifted on and up the big stairs. I looked vaguely at wonderful jewels and pottery and glassware. Every single piece must have been looted from somewhere where it was incredibly important, perhaps the greatest thing that had ever been made in each particular place. I wished, as I always did, that I knew more about, knew *anything* about, what made them important, how they fitted in.

'Where's Assyria?' asked Henry.

'Christ knows,' I said.

On to the mummies, of course.

'Look,' said Horace, 'a mummy of a cat. And look here, a mouse. That's an amazingly small mummy.'

We all flagged after that and made our way back to the entrance, past things we had already looked at. It was November, and though the pavement was covered with huge, blotchy red leaves from whatever the trees are out-side the British Museum, the sun was shining, and it was warm and clear, more like spring than late autumn. Henry, jokingly, I think, suggested that we walk home, but Horace agreed so enthusiastically that we had no choice but to set off on foot. I put my arm through Henry's and I felt as if we were a real grown-up family, walking all together past other families who were on holiday in London or perhaps just taking advantage of this fragile sunshine.

But Horace, the born-again hiker supreme, was inde-
fatigable. Henry and I smiled at each other as we watched
him striding ahead determinedly, heedless of our presence
and the occasional stare from a passer-by. He might have
been on his own.